Swoons for the Tangled series

T

"Do you see how he's looking at her on that cover? Look closer if you have to. That look on his face tells every Drew Girl what she needs to know: *Tied* is sublimely irreverent, massively sexy, and so frigging perfect readers will be bursting with giddy smiles. This, praise Emma, is the ending we all wanted."

—*New York Times* and *USA Today* author Christina Lauren

Tamed

"Witty, endearing, laugh-out-loud funny. Emma Chase doesn't disappoint."

—K. Bromberg, bestselling author of *Driven*

Twisted

"Hot, hilarious, and passionate. A great escape."

—Katy Evans, *New York Times* bestselling author of *Real* and *Mine*

"A delicious treat . . . funny, witty, and very sexy."

—*The Book Bella*

"I laughed. I cried. I yelled. I wanted to stop reading, but I couldn't. . . . Emma Chase really knows how to evoke emotion from her readers!"

—*Harlequin Junkie*

"Emma Chase grabbed me from page one and put me through the wringer."

—*Caffeinated Book Reviewer*

"A book that I couldn't wait to read and as I did, my emotions ran the gamut of hopeful, sad, with a dash of devastation and ultimately a great big pot of glee."

—*The Sub Club Books*

"Ms. Chase's writing style . . . is quick and smartass-y and yet there is depth to her characters."

—*Straight Shootin' Book Reviews*

"A yummy read for me . . . interesting, intense, sexy, and challenging."

—*Literary Cravings*

"In my wildest dreams, I never would have thought this story would reach the depths it did; the emotions and reactions it achieved. . . . I was obliterated, gutted, and slowly but surely put back together again."

—*Books to Breathe*

"Is emotional whiplash considered a sickness? I am more in love with this series than I was before, my heart just took a severe beating along the way."

—*The Geekery Book Review*

Tangled

"Well-written, clever, and charming."

—*Maryse's Book Blog*

"Total stop, drop, and roll reading. It goes fast so take a little time today to gobble this one up. You won't be sorry you did. Oh, and the sex . . . completely and utterly scandalicious."

—*Scandalicious Book Reviews*

Chapter 1

One week earlier

The apartment is silent. Still. The kind of quiet that can only be found in the predawn hours when the sky is dark and gray. The place has changed since you saw it last. Take a look around. Sterilized sippy cups lie in wait on a countertop; a green-cushioned, wooden high chair sits in the corner of the kitchen. Framed photographs clutter the walls and shelves.

Some are of Kate and me, but most of the captured images are of a dark-haired two-year-old, with brown, soulful eyes and a devilish smile.

Cut to the bedroom. Two bodies writhe on the bed, partially covered by rumpled silk sheets; my hips rotate in long, slow circles. I think the missionary position has gotten a bad rap. It's not boring. It allows the guy to take control—set the pace. To reach all those secret spots that make women moan and dig their fingernails into our shoulder blades.

Kind of like Kate is doing right now.

My head dips and I grasp one perky nipple with my lips, suctioning hard and flicking with my tongue. Kate arches her back. Her chin rises and her mouth opens, but no sound comes out. Her thighs squeeze harder, her pussy clenches tighter.

Even with the birth of a child on its résumé, Kate's cooch is just as snug and feels just as amazing as it did that first time. *God bless you, Dr. Kegel.*

My hips speed up and change their trajectory, thrusting to and fro in hard, quick strokes. When I know she can't take it anymore, I cover her mouth with mine, muffling her blissful cry. As much as I crave the sound of Kate's voice, these days it's all about staying quiet. Covert.

Why? you ask.

Let's pause here a minute and I'll explain.

It's our golden rule. Our first commandment: Don't wake the fucking baby.

I'll repeat that in case you missed it:

DON'T WAKE THE FUCKING BABY.

Like . . . *ever*.

Still don't get it? Must not have kids then. See, children are beautiful. Precious. Angelic. Particularly when they're asleep. If they're disturbed mid-sleep-cycle, however? They're monsters. Irritable, angry little beasts who bear a striking resemblance to gremlins fed after midnight.

And the cold truth is, even when they're well rested, babies are pretty frigging selfish. Self-centered and demanding. They don't care what you were doing before they needed you, or—more important—*whom* you were trying to do. They only care about themselves. *They're* hungry. *They're* wet. *They* want you to pick them up because the view from the crib has gotten old.

For all you happy couples out there awaiting the arrival of your own darling little cockblocker? I'm gonna tell you how it really is—not the utopian bullshit they feed you in those *What to Expect* books.

Here it goes: In the days after they're born, when you're still in the hospital, all infants do is sleep. I think the numbers are like twenty-three out of a twenty-four-hour day. I think they're slipping something into those bottles in the nursery.

Anyway, after a day or two, if all goes well, the hospital sends you home. And that's when the baby decides that it's slept enough. And finds something else to do to pass the time.

Did you know an infant's cry is twenty decibels higher than a train whistle? I shit you not. Look it up if you don't believe me.

By day three, I was convinced something was wrong with James. Maybe he had a gastrointestinal disorder. Maybe he was allergic to the wallpaper.

Maybe he just didn't fucking like us.

Whatever the reason, he was not a happy camper. And he was all too eager to let us know it. In the morning. In the afternoon. And—his favorite—all through the night.

Once in a while, just to screw with us, he'd mix it up and pass out for a while. But if he was awake? Yep—he was bawling. And I'm not talking about lip-quivering whimpers, either. Hell no. I'm talking lung-expanding, arm-and-leg-kicking, banshee-like screeching.

Shaken baby syndrome? I totally get that now.

Not that we were gonna go nuclear on his ass, but honestly? It wasn't fun.

My mother came over a lot, and at first I was relieved. I figured she'd done this twice before, she'd know how to fix him. Moms always make everything better.

Only . . . she didn't.

All she did was smile in that infuriatingly calm way while she bounced our squawking newborn on her shoulder. Then she'd tell us it was *normal.* That *all* babies cried. That Kate and I just had to figure out our *own* way of doing things.

I'd never before had the urge to strangle my mother. I'd never understood psychos like the Menendez brothers or Jim Gordon. But in those dark days when sleep—and blow jobs—were a distant memory, I'm sorry to say matricide was looking pretty damn attractive.

Because I was sure my mother knew the secrets of a happy baby—that she held the Keys to the Kingdom in her grasp. But for some evil, vengeful reason, she just wasn't handing them the fuck over. And sleep deprivation *can* drive you crazy. Even the most absurd ideas suddenly look like viable options.

One time, it was around four in the morning and I . . .

Actually, it might be better if I just show you, so you can get the full effect. Yes, it's a flashback within a flashback—but you're smart, you can handle it. I'll speak slowly, just in case:

James, five days old:

"Whaaa, whaaa, whaaa, whaaa."

In the time it takes my eyes to crack open and interpret the numbers on the alarm clock, Kate is already sitting up, ready to spring out of bed and scoop up the swaddled ball of angry in the bassinet beside the bed.

Four a.m.

Mentally, I groan—because it's been less than an hour since he fell asleep. Although my first egotistical instinct is to close my eyes and let Kate deal with it, the part of me that wants to help out while I can—because I don't want her to lose her mind—backhands the selfish part.

"Whaaaaaaa, whaaaaaaaa."

"I got him, Kate." I toss the covers off and slip on a pair of sweats. "Go back to sleep." I'm kind of hoping she fights me over it . . . but she doesn't. She flops back down against the pillow.

I pick James up and hold him against my bare chest. His cheek nuzzles my skin before he unleashes a heartbroken cry. I walk out of the bedroom with him to the kitchen. From the fridge I grab a bottle of breast milk, which Kate filled this afternoon with that weird dairy-cow pump thing she got from Delores at the baby shower. Holding James with one hand, I run the bottle under hot water the way the lactation adviser at the hospital instructed us to do.

After it's warmed, I make my way to the living room with bleary eyes and tired, wobbly legs. I sit on the couch, cradling James in my arms, and run the nipple across his lips.

I realize it's a bad idea to feed him every time he wakes. I know all about the importance of a feeding schedule and burping and teaching him to "self-soothe." I understand he shouldn't actually be hungry, since he just ate an hour ago. But sleep deprivation is a torture technique for a reason. So all that crap goes right out the window, in the hopes of getting him—and me—back to sleep as quickly as possible.

He takes two drags on the bottle, then rejects it, turning his head with an openmouthed squawk: "Whaaaaaaa."

I look up at the ceiling and curse God.

"What do you want, James?" My voice has a frustrated edge. "You're dry, I'm holding you, I'm trying to feed you—what the hell do you want?" I walk back to the kitchen and grab the checkbook off the counter.

"Will money make you happy?"

Ridiculous—yes, I know. Don't judge me.

"I'll give you ten thousand dollars for four hours of sleep. I'll

write the check out right now." I wave the checkbook in front of his face, hoping to distract him.

It just pisses him off more.

"Whaaaaaa . . ."

I toss the checkbook back on the counter and return to the living room. Then I pace the floor, rocking him softly in my arms, patting his ass. You know I must be really desperate—because I try singing:

Hush, little baby, don't say a word
Daddy's gonna buy you a . . .

I stop—because why the fuck would any baby want a mockingbird? None of those nursery rhymes make any goddamn sense. I don't know any other lullabies, so I go for the next best thing, "Enter Sandman" by Metallica:

Take my hand,
We're off to never-never land . . .

"Whaaaaaaaaaaaaaa."

When that doesn't help, I sit down on the couch. I lay James on my thighs and support his head with my hand. I look into his little face—and even though he's still bawling, I can't help but smile. Then, in a low, calm voice, I talk to him.

"I get it, you know. Why you're so unhappy. One minute you're floating in amniotic fluid—it's dark and warm and quiet. Then a minute later, you're freezing and there's bright lights and some asshole is pricking your heel with a needle. Your whole world is turned upside down."

The tide of tears starts to recede. Though there's a sporadic whimper, for the most part his big, brown eyes keep contact with mine. Interested in what I'm saying. I know the accepted theory is that babies have no understanding of language at this stage, but—like men attempting to get out of household chores—I think they know more than they let on.

"I felt the same way when I met your mother. There I was, cruising along, making the most of a fan-fucking-tastic life—and your mom came along and shot it all to hell. I didn't know which way was up—with work, with my Saturday nights. This is a talk for another time, but it's true what they say: you spend nine months trying to get out, and the rest of your life trying to work your way back in."

I chuckle at my own joke. "You probably don't want to hear this, but your mom is gorgeous—the finest ass I've ever laid eyes on. Still, I really liked my old life and I couldn't imagine anything better. But I was wrong, James—falling in love with her, earning her trust, having you, are the best things I've ever done."

He's not crying at all anymore but simply regarding me with quiet attention. "The adjustment might be hard . . . but it's worth it. So could you cut us some slack, please? We love you so much—I can't wait to show you how fucking great life is on the outside. And you don't have to be scared, because we'll keep you warm and fed. And I promise I'll never, ever let anything bad happen to you."

His little mouth opens in a stretching yawn. And his eyes slow-blink. I stand up and pace the room again—slowly.

Kate's hushed voice comes from the across the room. "You certainly have a way with words, Mr. Evans." Her hair is wild, messy; my college T-shirt is baggy on her and almost reaches her knees.

"What are you doing up?" I ask.

She shrugs. "I couldn't fall back asleep. And I heard you whispering out here." She walks up to us and rests her head against my arm—gazing down at the baby. "He's asleep."

And so he is.

"Do I risk putting him down, or should I learn to sleep standing up like a frigging horse?"

Kate loops her arm through mine and guides me to the couch. She sits and pats the spot next to her. Like a member of the bomb squad handling a device with a hair trigger, I shift James so he's on my chest, his head resting on the steady beat of my heart. Then I sit down and put my feet on the table and my head against the back cushion and my arm around Kate's shoulders.

I sigh. "God, that feels good."

Still not better than sex—I don't give a shit what the new-mom magazines say. Sleep is good, but screwing will always be better.

Kate curls her feet under her and rests her head against my arm. "It sure does."

A few moments later, all three of us are sound asleep.

It's possible James understood my offer of bribery, because that night he slept there on my chest for three whole hours. Before he woke up—and it started all over again.

But I have a theory. I think it's all deliberate. I think God plans for those first days home with a new baby to suck donkey balls. Because afterward? Everything else—the shitty diapers, the regurgitation, the constant changing of clothes and bed linens, teething—they all feel like a walk in the park.

After a few more days, I realized my mother wasn't just being a bitch. She was actually giving us solid advice. Because together, Kate and I were able to figure it all out.

You know how dogs have a bark that says, *Let me out or I'll piss on your recliner*? And another that says, *Just give me the squeaky toy, you sadistic son of a bitch*? And even another one that says, *I'm not playing. I'm literally going to chew your face off now*?

Babies aren't much different from dogs. There's a cry when they're hungry. One when they're tired. Another one when they're bored, or when maybe their nose itches and they just don't have the manual dexterity to scratch.

In any case, once you figure out the Language of Crying Baby? Life is a whole lot sweeter. And quieter.

Plus—here's the kicker—in spite of the exhaustion? The frustration? The crying that makes you want to puncture your fucking eardrum with a meat thermo?

You love them anyway. Fully. Fiercely.

Intensely.

You wouldn't change a thing about them—wouldn't trade them for all the freaking iPhones in China. Sounds strange, I know. But that's just how it is.

Screw the Peace Corps. Parenthood is the toughest job you'll ever love.

So now, two years later, back to the porn-worthy sex . . .

I slide my hands under Kate's ass—kneading and lifting—bringing us closer. Rocking us faster. My forehead hovers close to hers and I open my eyes. So I can watch.

I'm greedy like that. I want to soak up every gasp—every flicker of pleasure that dances across her exquisite face. Pleasure *I'm* giving her.

I know Kate's body as well as I know my own. There's a contentment, a confidence, a power, in that knowledge that I can't fully explain. We're completely in sync. Joined body and soul. A well-lubed machine working in tandem toward that moment of pure, hot paradise that I've only ever experienced with her.

Kate's breathing changes. It turns panting and desperate, and I know she's close. Sweat trickles down my chest. I move harder, grinding against her—inside her—with every forward push. Warms sparks tickle my spine and tighten my balls. Heat spreads down and out until every nerve in my body is shaking. Quivering. Begging to explode.

Sweet Jesus.

My hips rock back, and I pull almost all the way out. Then, for a second, I freeze. We teeter right on the edge. Together. Savoring the sensation of that perfect moment—right before you come—where it feels so fucking good. But you know it's about to feel even better.

I slam my cock inside her, burying deep as Kate's hips jerk upward. She spasms hard around me, gripping me tight over and over, while ecstasy wracks my body, making me shudder.

I hold on to Kate's ass as if my life depends on it. I press my lips against her neck to soften the sounds I can't control. "Kate . . . Kate . . . fuck . . . Kate . . ."

It's astounding. Fantastic. But not unusual. 'Cause we're just that frigging good together.

I exhale harshly against Kate's skin as I come back down to earth. But I don't move yet. I just don't have the will. I'm considering going back to sleep. On top of her.

She won't mind.

At least that's what I think, until Kate performs the move that seems to amuse every woman on earth. And causes every man on earth to want to squeal like an impaled pig. Without warning, she uses her powerful pussy muscles to squeeze my *extremely* sensitive dick.

Guys *hate* that. We don't think it's funny. Kate knows this.

I jerk back, pull out, and roll off her.

I try to look annoyed—but don't quite pull it off. Because Kate's eyes are sparkling. And she's giggling. And she looks so messy-haired, flushed-faced, just-fucked beautiful, that it's impossible not to grin back.

She knows that too.

I whisper, "Hi."

"Hey."

I turn on my back and Kate scoots closer, resting her head on my chest and her palm on my stomach.

My tattoo? Noticed that, did you? Yeah—I got another one right after James was born. It's straightforward, nothing flashy. But it's as meaningful as Kate's name on my right arm.

It simply says *James*. Right over my heart.

"So," Kate starts, "big day today, huh?"

I run my fingers through her hair. "No. Next week is a big day. Today's just a technicality."

One hundred sixty-eight hours. Eight thousand six hundred and forty minutes.

Not that I'm counting or anything.

That's when it'll be official. That's when Kate Brooks is gonna marry me. When she'll not only sleep in my bed because she wants to—but because she's legally obligated to be there.

Husband and wife. Flesh of my flesh. What God has joined together, let no one who wants to keep his arm attached try to pull asunder.

Kate bites her lip. "Have the guys told you what the plan is?"

She's referring to the bachelor party. My bachelor party.

My *Las Vegas* bachelor party.

The stag party is a night to celebrate the demise of a man's singlehood, in the rankest, most depraved manner possible. Sex and alcohol are big themes. You've seen the movies—*The Hangover*, *Bachelor Party* . . . it's the last hurrah. Like the night before you ship off to war or, if you're a woman, start a diet.

The groom is expected to gorge himself on all the stuff he supposedly won't be getting anymore, once he slips that ring on his bride's pretty little finger.

Of course, Kate is not the average bride. And because our relationship—and our sex life—is better now than it's ever been, at first I didn't want a party. I just didn't see the point.

For a few men, such as me, once you're in love, all the other tits and asses in the world just sort of . . . blend together. It's like . . . cars in the city—the honking, the revving, the screech of tires on blacktop. I hear them, I know they're there, but I just don't give a shit. I don't glance their way, don't stop to look. Not anymore—because I've got a top-of-the-line classic in my garage, just waiting for me to come home and ride her.

She's the only one I want.

But eventually, the guys convinced me. Jack, Matthew, and Steven cornered me in the conference room and explained that the bachelor party wasn't really for me. It was for all the other guys, who actually had to work to get laid.

Meaning the single guys and . . . you know . . . the ones who are already married.

After hearing them plead their case, I was on board. Between work, Kate, and the adorable little dictator that is our son, I haven't had a lot of quality time with the boys. I figured it would be a good time—a night of bonding—a way to make some lifelong memories with my closest friends.

So when Kate asks if the guys have told me what the plan is, I answer, "Not really." Matthew's exact words were *"The less you know, the better. Plausible deniability."* But I don't want to tell Kate that. It'll just make her worry.

She doesn't let it go, however. "Well, if you had to guess, what do you think you'll do?"

I shrug again. "Steak dinner, casino, drinking . . ."

"Strippers?"

Did you hear the change in her voice? The preemptive anger? The bite?

My eyebrows rise. "A visit to a strip club will probably be on the itinerary, yeah."

She scoffs. In that you're-such-a-prick kind of way. Then she sits up and crosses her arms. "Of course. Figures. Because you haven't spent enough time in the company of strippers—you have to squeeze in another night's worth before our wedding."

Have you ever heard of the Missile Defense System—the MDS? Started by Reagan in the eighties, its sole purpose is to defend against another country's attack. To destroy their missiles before impact. To deflect damage. The system doesn't analyze the opposition's argument. It doesn't take the time to consider that maybe they have a valid *reason* for attacking. It simply reacts. Immediately. Defensively.

"Don't get pissy—it's a bachelor party. Are you trying to tell me Dee-Dee's not gonna have a guy . . . or ten . . . shaking their junk in your face?"

Did I not mention that the girls will be coming along on our weekend adventure? They are. Delores thought it'd be fun to make it a group excursion, then split up for our separate nights of debauchery. I thought it was a fabulous suggestion—made me *almost* like Dee.

"That's different and you know it," Kate argues.

"Except it's really not."

"Will it bother you if Dee hired strippers?"

For years, Sister B told us there were no stupid questions. Boy, was she full of shit.

The mere thought of a half-naked guy who isn't me grinding on Kate? It makes me want to destroy something—like a face. Go all *Fight Club* and break someone into mangled, bloody pieces until he'll never resemble a human being again.

Maybe it's caveman. Maybe it's irrational and sexist and unfair. But that's just how I am.

"Of course it'll fucking bother me!"

"Dee-Dee says what's good for the goose is good for the gander."

"Matthew needs to learn how to muzzle his fucking gander."

"Like you muzzle me?"

I can be biting too. "No, sweetheart—I enjoy your mouth way too much to muzzle it. I prefer it wide-open and waiting."

Kate gasps, and I expect her to come back at me, guns blazing. Because this is what we do. You've been around long enough—you know the drill. It's foreplay, afterplay, it's jabs and zingers. They're just words—a way to vent our frustrations or turn each other on.

They don't mean jack shit. Only on rare occasions is there any real anger or hurt feelings behind them. And this isn't one of those times.

Only . . . apparently it is.

"See—this is exactly what I was afraid of. We haven't even left yet, and you're already being a bastard. I *knew* this would happen again."

Kate turns slightly away from me, shaking her head stiffly. That's when I see them. Tears. Welling in her eyes, ready to fall, being held back by her sheer stubbornness alone.

I'm surprised. And aching. Like I got shot in the heart with a rock-size rubber bullet.

Kate throws the sheets off and moves to get out of bed. But

I'm faster—Flash Gordon can eat my dust. Before her feet hit the floor, I'm in front of her, hands up. Remorseful and apologetic.

And naked.

When you're trying to plead your case? Being naked doesn't hurt.

"Kate . . . wait . . . just slow down. Back up a minute." I grab for her wrist.

But she pulls away. "Stop touching me!"

Right—like *that's* gonna happen.

But I don't get a chance to tell her that. A dreaded sound echoes across the room and halts all action, grabbing our full attention. Because it's coming from the baby monitor.

It's a rustling, the sound of cotton rubbing cotton. Like snipers in the jungle, we don't move a muscle. We don't say a word. We wait. Until the rustling stops. And all is quiet again.

That was a warning sign—a shot across our bow. A "shut the hell up."

We don't have to be told twice.

What ensues next is a comical soundless argument only true parents will understand. It's all mouthing and miming, facial expression and hand flailing. Until eventually, Kate flips me the finger.

Then I smile. And mouth, "Okay."

I mean, if she's ready for round two, who am I to deny her?

I tackle her. We roll around on the bed for a minute until I pin her down—sitting on her waist—trapping her hands over her head. The physical exertion defuses some of the tension, and Kate looks a little less devastated. When I'm sure she won't try to escape, I grab the comforter and pull it over both of us, so we're shielded in a conversation-muting cocoon.

I flop down on my side facing Kate, and in a half-whispered

tone I get right to the point. "If the idea of strippers being part of the entertainment bothers you so much, why the hell did you say it was okay to have my bachelor party in Las Vegas?"

Strippers in Las Vegas are like corn in Iowa. They're kind of what the city is known for.

Kate squirms. Then she sighs. "Because everyone was so excited about going to Las Vegas. I didn't want to be the downer. Bachelor and bachelorette parties in Vegas are like . . . tradition, right?"

Not too long ago, sacrificing goats was a tradition too. Doesn't make it a good idea.

"Not all traditions have to be followed. If you're really that uncomfortable about it, I'll tell the guys no. We'll stick to gambling, cigars, and alcohol."

She pauses a moment—thinking. "You would do that for me?"

I chuckle. Because by now, how can she not know? "Of course I would."

Kate tucks her hands under her cheek. It makes her look young, vulnerable. My chest tightens with the desire to protect her. From anything—everything—that could cause her pain.

Including my own tongue.

"I don't really care about the strippers, Drew."

Now I'm confused. "Are you saying that because you really don't care—or because you think that's what I want you to say?"

I have to ask, because in my experience, women will tell you to do something and then slit your fucking throat when you actually do it. Since you were supposed to know they didn't *really* want you to do it. That they don't *really* mean what they say.

Except for the times when they do.

It's like an undiscovered form of schizophrenia. God gave you a mouth for a reason, ladies. Well . . . several reasons actually.

But the point is—use it. Be up-front. It'll save us all a lot of time and energy.

"No—I'm being honest. Now that I know you don't want to go to a strip club, it doesn't bother me so much if you do."

"Then why were you upset?"

"I think, deep down, I'm just . . . afraid."

"Of what?"

"You."

Ouch. Gotta say, that one kind of hurts. Like an old knee injury that acts up so infrequently, you almost forget it's there. Until it reminds you. And you're bedridden for a week.

Kate sees my expression and elaborates. "I'm afraid you're going to do something . . . that you're going to see something, or hear something, and that you'll take it the wrong way. That there'll be a misunderstanding, and you'll react . . . badly."

I rub my eyes. And sigh. "I thought we were past all that, Kate."

She grabs my hand and squeezes. "We *are* past it. We forgave each other, and we're so good now. But . . . you have to admit . . . there's a pattern."

Rose Kennedy once declared, *"It has been said, 'Time heals all wounds.' I do not agree. The wounds remain. In time, the mind, protecting its sanity, covers them with scar tissue and the pain lessens. But it is never gone."*

Preaching to the choir, Rosie. Preaching to the choir . . .

My hand trails out and cups Kate's cheek to reassure her. "I'm not that guy anymore, Kate."

Okay, you're right: deep down I *am* still that guy. But I'm smarter now. *More.* I'm a father. In a week, I'll be a husband. And

I would cut my dick off before I would ever hurt Kate like that again.

I've grown, God damn it.

"I love you, Kate. And I trust you. I trust us. We talk about things—I don't just react now. So I'm not gonna screw this up. Not this weekend; not ever again."

Oh, irony. You ugly bitch.

Kate's hand covers mine. She stares into my eyes, looking for truth or sincerity or I don't know what. Whatever it is, she finds it. Because she smiles. And kisses me softly. "I believe you."

Then she pulls back and asks, "Would you feel better if I tell Dee to cancel any stripper plans she may have made for us?"

Yes.

"No."

Hell yes.

"Well . . . maybe."

Yes, yes, yes, yes, yes, yes, yes, yes, yes, yes, yes, yes, yes, yes, yes, yes, yes, yes, yes.

"No. No. I want you to have fun with the girls. You know, do what ganders do."

See? If that's not evidence of fucking growth, I don't know what the hell is. Besides, male strippers aren't that big a deal. Because most of them are aspiring dancers. And we all know what that means. . . .

Anyway, no girl wants to bang a guy in a banana hammock. I don't care if you're built like a brick shithouse and hung like a freaking horse—if you're wearing a man-thong? You look like a tool.

As we sit up, Kate tells me, "Watching a greased-up guy shaking his ass is not really my idea of fun, Drew." She wiggles her eyebrows my way. "Now, *you* greased up and dancing, on the other hand, that sounds like a good time."

This is why I love her.

"You're the perfect woman."

I pull her in for a kiss—longer than the last one. But just as our tongues come out to play, a small voice chirps out from the monitor.

"Mummy? Daaaddy? Up-o. Up-o."

I pull back. "The beast has risen. You shower first, I'll get him."

"Okay."

I slide on a pair of sweats as Kate pulls some clothes from the drawer.

"Daaddy! Mummy! Up-o. Up-o. Up-o!"

My son is not a big fan of patience. Wonder where he gets that from?

"Oh, and Drew?"

I turn toward Kate. "Yeah?"

"My grandmother used to say, 'Look with your eyes, not with your hands.' When you're at that strip bar? Make sure you do that."

I nod. "Got it, boss." I stride forward and grab her chin, freeing her lip from her teeth's grip. Then I kiss it better—making her just a little dazed and confused. "Stop fucking worrying. We're gonna have a great time with our friends this weekend. Nothing bad is gonna happen. I promise."

Famous last words, right? How's that for a jinx? *Idiot.*

I spin her back around and slap both cheeks with one hand. "Now get that ass in the shower before I decide to tap it again."

Kate laughs, 'cause she thinks I'm kidding. Only—

"Daaadddyyy! Up-o! Up-o!"

Right. Duty calls. Kate heads for the bathroom, and I go to spring James from his cage.

So that's how it started. Everything was awesome. We were talking. Laughing. Communicating.

Fucking.

It was like a fairy tale, for Christ's sake.

Did you ever notice how fairy tales all start off great? The beautiful princess, the happy kingdom? Then it all turns to shit. One minute Hansel's feeling no pain, chomping on a window made of sugar, and the next minute some old hag is trying to shove his ass in an oven.

For any of you out there who still think I'm an unworthy, self-absorbed douche? I have a feeling you're going to enjoy this.

A lot.

Chapter 2

James's room is dim. The shades are drawn and the only illumination comes from a Buzz Lightyear night-light in the corner. It's the mother of all boy's rooms. Yellow and green? No thanks. The walls are navy and cream, the furniture dark cherrywood. A toddler-size basketball net is against one wall, and a full-size train table against the other. A comfy rocking chair is stationed between two arched windows, with a well-worn copy of *Goodnight Moon* lying in wait on the seat. Framed pictures of family—and the new Yankee Stadium—hang on the walls. A Metallica poster is taped to the back of the door.

I wanted it front and center but Kate shot me down.

James's big, dark eyes light up when I walk in. He's the perfect mini-me—his nose, his chin, his black hair that sticks up at all angles.

"Morning, buddy."

He holds on to the rail of his crib and bounces like a cotton-clad chimpanzee.

His words are carefully pronounced, with stresses on the consonants. Kind of like a robot. "Hel-lo, Dad-dee."

So fucking cute.

I pick him up, hold him high, and nibble on his belly, making him shriek. Then I bring him back down and give him a squeeze. His head turns and rests on my shoulder, and his breath tickles my neck. I kiss his hair again—just because I can.

I'll never understand those guys who refuse to hug and kiss their kids—particularly their *male* kids. Coldhearted pricks, if you ask me. The idea that too much affection can make a boy soft is a big steaming pile of crap.

If you want your kid to be confident—secure? You have to give them a good foundation—set the right example. Take my old man, for instance. I grew up knowing he was fully capable of kicking my ass whenever I stepped out of line. Which he did. Frequently. But he also showed me every day that he had my back. That he loved me, was proud of everything I did or tried to do. James is gonna grow up the exact same way.

A rancid aroma invades my nose. "Jesus, James." I lay him on the table to get him changed.

You look surprised. You shouldn't be. Real men change diapers.

I'm thinking about putting that on a T-shirt.

In fact, anything Kate can do—bath time, bedtime, midnight feedings—I can do too. I kind of have to.

Kate was only twenty-eight when James was born. For a professional in our field, that's young. And as happy as she was to do the mom thing—and despite a boatload of guilt—she just wasn't ready to trade in the corporate ladder for Mommy and Me's and goddamn *Wiggles* songs.

A nanny or day care was out of the question. When I was young, I didn't even like to board our dogs. No way was I handing my kid off to some strangers, hoping every day that they didn't cause harm.

But I did promise Kate—once upon a time—that I'd make all her dreams come true. So, we compromised. Here's how that played out. You'll find the ending of this exchange particularly gratifying . . . or at least I did:

James—four weeks old.

It's ten thirty by the time I walk through the door of our apartment. These may seem like late hours to you, but in the field of investment banking, it's pretty much par for the course. One seven o'clock meeting runs over, then a conference call with Indonesia, a couple more hours spent reviewing contracts, and here we are.

When James was first born, I took two weeks dad-ternity leave, but now I'm back at the office full speed ahead. Kate's doing the stay-at-home-mom thing. We used to alternate the middle-of-the-night feeding shifts, but because it's difficult to form a coherent sentence—let alone manage millions of dollars—when half your brain is asleep, they now fall on her, so I can get a night of decent shut-eye and not decimate my clients' fortunes.

I toss my keys on the table and nudge the door closed with my foot. I step into the living room—Kate's sitting on the couch with a basket of laundry at her feet, folding tiny pants that will join their onesie brethren stacked on the table. Her long, soft hair—which I relish feeling draped across my thighs—is tied up in a bun. She's wearing short pajama shorts and a navy T-shirt, and I can't help but notice her still-larger-than-normal-from-breast-feeding tits are free from the usual bra constraints.

Bonus.

In a louder voice than I'd intended, I say, "Hey, beautiful."

"Shhh!" She attacks. "If you wake that baby, I'll pluck out every pubic hair you have the next time you fall asleep."

My eyes widen. She's been spending way too much time with Delores these days.

I lower my voice. "Sorry." I sit beside her on the couch and lean over for a kiss.

My lips coax a smile from her—as usual. "Hi," she greets me in a much-happier-to-see-me tone. "Do you want me to heat you up a plate?"

"Nah, I'll just make myself a bowl of cereal."

Kate yawns as she picks up a my mom is hotter than your mom *bib and continues to fold.*

"Rough day?" I ask.

"Not so much. He was just really cranky around six—it took me forever to get him down for the night."

I nod. Then tilt my head toward the hallway. "I'm just gonna go check on him."

Kate shoots me down. "No—no, you're not."

"I'll be really quiet."

"Drew—"

"I won't even touch him."

Wryly she points out, "We both know you're incapable of seeing James and not touching him."

Touché.

"And then he'll be up and I'll have to feed him to get him back down. And his whole schedule will be blown for the night."

I see the wisdom of what she's saying. Doesn't mean I have to frigging like it.

"I haven't seen him all day!" I had to run out the door earlier than usual this morning, to make a meeting with a client uptown.

"It's not healthy for a baby to go days without laying eyes on the man who fathered him."

I don't know if this is a fact—but it sounds good, so I stick with it.

Again, Kate's not having it. "He's four weeks old. He needs a schedule more than he needs to see his daddy."

I frown. I think my feelings are hurt. "That's a fucked-up thing to say."

She shrugs. "Doesn't make it any less true."

I sigh. And decide on a more subversive course of action. "Then I'll just go make that bowl of cereal."

Kate watches me as I get up. Then softly calls to my retreating back, "Stay away from the nursery, Drew—don't even look at the door."

I neither agree nor disagree. Even though Kate and I have been together for years, loopholes still apply. I enter the kitchen, grab the milk out of the fridge, and pour myself a bowl Lucky Charms. I take two bites and—

Did you hear that? It sounded like a baby's cry, didn't it?

No?

Then I recommend you get your hearing checked, 'cause I definitely heard it.

I slip through the kitchen door and stealthily make my way down the hall to the nursery. The door is cracked a few inches—just wide enough to stick my head in. The night-light casts a warm glow on the dark wood furniture, rocking chair, and stuffed animals stacked in the corner. I listen. And all I hear is the sound of James's deep, rhythmic baby breathing.

Guess it wasn't a cry I heard, after all. But . . . since I'm here and all, it won't hurt to have a peek, right? Right.

Like a kid sneaking downstairs before sunrise on Christmas morning, I step softly into the room. I stand next to the crib and gaze down at my sleeping boy. An instant smile appears on my face. Because he's so goddamn adorable.

He's on his back, head turned to the right, one fisted little hand bent at the elbow above his dark-haired head. He's dressed in a cotton, feet-covering, dark-green romper. I can't resist running my finger across his plump, baby-soft cheek.

He doesn't flinch or stir. So I continue to look at him—and it's kind of crazy how entertaining it is just watching him breathe.

After I've had my fill, I take one step toward the door.

Then something fucking dreadful happens.

You had *to have seen this coming.*

Yep, James's head turns to the left, and his feet kick out and his sweet features scrunch up. Then—like a baby bird fresh out of the egg—he lets out a cry.

"Whaaaaa."

My eyes snap to the door, then back to him, as the second squawk leaves his lips.

"Whaaaaaaa."

"Shit. Shhh," I whisper. "James . . ." I rub his belly. "Shhh, go back to sleep."

Of course, that does a whole lot of nothing.

"Whhaaaaaaaaa."

Screw it. I pick him up and bounce him against my shoulder. "You gotta be quiet, buddy. If your mom finds me in here, she's gonna lock up her pussy like a steel safe. It'll take me hours to crack that bad boy back open."

Technically, the safe is closed for maintenance anyway. We still have two weeks to go before the doctor will give us the green light. Until then, there's a strict "Thou shalt not pass" policy. I'm not even allowed to make her cum with my mouth, or the ever-so-popular-with-teenagers dry-humping method. Roberta said her uterus needed to recoup, which means no orgasmic spasming permitted.

That being said, you get my analogy. My son, on the other hand, does not. Or he just doesn't fucking care.

"Whaaa, whaaa, whaaaaaaaa."

Then Kate's standing in the doorway, looking righteously pissed off. "Kiss the pubic hairs good-bye, Drew."

I chuckle. "What? I heard him crying—I just got here before you."

It doesn't count as a lie if the person you're lying to knows *it's a lie.*

She lets out an exasperated sigh and reaches for the baby. "Give him to me."

I tuck him against me and turn my body, like a football player trying to keep the ball from getting snatched in the pileup. "No, I got him. Go back to whatever you were doing."

"He won't settle down for you."

"And he'll never *settle down for me if you're the only one holding him all the time." I kiss the top of his screaming head. "I got this, Kate. Go take a bath or something."*

Isn't that what all new mothers want?

"Is that your way of telling me I smell?"

Guess not.

"No . . . I'm saying I stirred the shit, I'll deal with the stench."

Still looking unsure, she runs her hand down James's back. "All right. Just . . . holler if you need me."

I give her lips a peck. "We're good."

Finally she smiles, then she leaves.

Most men are inept when it comes to babies. Either from lack of experience or because they're afraid they're going to irreversibly screw something up. Give us an appliance that needs fixing, we'll take it apart, figure it out, and put it back together again, even if we're unfamiliar with it.

Babies? Not so easy to put back together.

And there's all these perils we have to be mindful of—soft spots, necks that can't support heads, nasty-looking belly buttons waiting to fall off . . . don't get me fucking started on the circumcision. Men aren't good multitaskers, remember?

So for most, infant care is an activity best left to the mothers.

Most—but not me. Because I cut my teeth on Mackenzie. When she was an infant, I wasn't around for the nighttime routine stuff, but I learned a lot about everything else. If a man can change a baby girl's diaper, there is nothing he can't accomplish. So, because I have her infancy under my belt, and because I'm pretty much awesome at anything I do, I'm not intimidated by James's crying. It's not a fun part of fatherhood—but I can deal.

I shift him from my shoulder to cradle him in my arms.

"Whaaa, whaaa, whaaa . . ."

"Hey, buddy, what's with the tears? You don't have to cry—I'm gonna have you back to sleep in no time."

I grab a pacifier off the dresser and tease it into his mouth. Whimpering, he gives it a few sucks before opening his mouth to screech because he realizes it's not the real thing. I catch it before it falls to the floor.

Then I sit in the rocking chair. "Yeah, I know it's not what you really want. And I don't blame you—your mom's boobs are spectacular. But . . . you gotta take what you can get. And right now, this little piece of plastic is the next best thing."

I slide it between his lips again, and this time he doesn't reject it. He sucks rapidly and his eyes fall closed for a moment before he drags them back open—a sure sign he's exhausted but fighting it. I rock slowly in the chair and tap his ass gently in a steady beat.

In a soothing whisper I tell him, "You want to hear what your old man did today? I set up a fifty-million-dollar acquisition for a man who invented a new app. He's kind of a tool. When you're older, you'll learn the world is full of tools. Anyway, this particular tool didn't think the deal was good enough, so Daddy had to explain to him why it was. First I showed him . . ."

You don't really want to hear the rest, do you? Suffice it to say, twenty minutes later, James was out cold. I kiss his forehead and lay him back in his crib. Then I go out to the living room looking for some quality time with my girlfriend. I find Kate on the couch, with a still-half-full basket of clothes next to her.

She doesn't acknowledge me right away—and she's not folding clothes anymore. She's holding a pair of baby socks in each hand, unnervingly staring off into space. In deep thought.

Usually for guys, when our women are contemplating something serious? It's a bad sign.

Cautiously I sit down next to her. "The baby's asleep."

Her blank expression doesn't change. "That's good."

"Kate? You okay?"

Snapping out of wherever she was, she turns to me quickly and tries to blow it off. "Oh, yeah. Yeah, I'm fine."

Fine*—a red flag if there ever was one.*

I don't waste time with pleasantries. "Fuck fine—what's wrong?"

She focuses her attention on the socks. "I just realized . . . this is my life now."

I try hard to decipher the hidden female message in that statement—and come up with zilch. "O-kay . . . and . . . ?"

"And folding clothes, dirty dishes, afternoon walks, naptimes, changing diapers . . . that's my life. That's what I have to look forward to."

"Well . . . changing diapers won't last forever. And in two more weeks I'll be able to make you cum again in numerous, illicit ways—that's something worth looking forward to."

That gets a chuckle out of her, but it's halfhearted. "I'm a terrible person."

I rub her shoulder. "If you're *a terrible person, I'm in some seriously deep shit."*

This time her smile is a bit more genuine. "I love James, Drew. Love *. . . isn't even a strong enough word . . ."*

I nod, because I and any parent know exactly what she means.

". . . and I know how lucky I am. Lots of women would kill to be able to stay home full-time with their kids. I really am grateful for the life I have—but I never thought this would be all I'd have."

And the tears start to fall. Big ones.

In the days after James's birth, he wasn't the only one on a bawling binge.

Kate was a mess.

I thought I understood the havoc hormones can wreak on the female personality—but I didn't understand jack. Pregnancy hormones are a whole other animal entirely. She cried because James was beautiful, she cried because she loved me so much, and because of how much I love her. She cried when James cried, and when he slept or if he sneezed. She cried because she hadn't lost all the baby weight two days after he was born, the way those motherfucking evil, narcissistic celebrities make women feel they should.

Even though I'm accustomed to my son's crying jags, seeing Kate cry will never be something I'm okay with.

My chest tightens, squeezing my heart as she wipes at her cheeks. "I feel so guilty for missing work—for watching you walk out that door in the morning and wishing it was me. How screwed up is that?"

I rub her back and tell her the truth: "It's not screwed up at all."

Kate looks at me with surprise in her eyes.

"I wouldn't want to quit my job, either—I'd be a miserable bas-

tard if I couldn't go to the office anymore." Then I ask, "Why didn't you say something sooner?"

"I thought it would pass, once I got used to being home—had a new routine going. But it's just gotten worse."

The strange thing is, I know just how she feels.

"To be honest, I'm not exactly thrilled with the arrangements we have now, either."

Thankfully, her tears have dried. The vise grip on my heart lessens. "You're not?"

I shake my head. "I'm missing all the good stuff. I go for days without seeing James awake even for a minute. It sucks ass. Like the other day, when he smiled for the first time."

She tries to make me feel better. "That was just gas, Drew."

"Of course it was, because boys think passing gas is funny."

"I sent you a video."

I shake my head. "That's not the same. At this rate, I'll miss everything—his first word, his first step, the first time he realizes he can aim and piss on things—all the big moments."

Kate takes my hand. "So . . . what are we talking about here? Are you saying you want to stay home part-time?"

Once the words are actually said, I realize that's what I've wanted all along. "And you'll work part-time. I'll go the office Monday, Wednesday, and Friday . . . because I'm still the frigging man in the relationship . . . and you'll do Tuesday and Thursday."

"Some of our clients aren't going to be good with that. Jefferson Industries' CEO is a prick—he'll have major issues."

Like I give a damn. "Whoever isn't okay with it, I'll make sure they stay in-house. Pass them off to Jack or Matthew—and if we lose a few, my father will get over it. Nepotism has its advantages, Kate. I say we fucking exploit them."

"Our bonuses will take a hit."

I shrug. "It's only money."

If you don't have a boatload of extraneous cash and investments lying around, I wouldn't recommend adopting this attitude. But since I do . . . I can.

Then I point out, "In six or seven years James will be in school, then we can both go back full-time. Unless we have a few more kids between now and then—and since the activity that gets them here is at the top of our Favorite Things to Do list, that's a definite possibility."

There's a light in her eyes that wasn't there when I came home. Knowing I help put it there makes me proud of myself—not that that's an unusual feeling, but in this case it's especially awesome.

Kate squeezes my hand enthusiastically. "So, we're doing this? We're really doing this?"

"You and I and James will go into the office tomorrow and have a sit-down with Dad, George, and Frank."

She throws herself at me—chest to chest, arms around my neck, legs straddling my thighs. "I'm so excited!"

"As excited as you are about getting the go-ahead from Roberta in two weeks?"

Kate squints. "Ah . . . not that excited—but very close."

And then we're kissing—tongues dancing and tasting. I fall back on the couch, taking her with me—keeping her on top.

Her lips tease their way to my ear. "I love you," Kate breathes, before licking around the shell. Heated lust gathers in my gut, then furrows out to my thighs and arms—and my dick.

I return the sentiment. "I love you."

Kate's mouth lowers to my neck, torturous in its feather-light brushes against my skin. "And I love our life."

My hand tangles in her hair, loosening the bun, making it fall. "Me too."

She drops to her knees on the floor and I sit up, legs spread so she can nestle between my thighs. She looks up at me with hungry, dark eyes and a naughty-girl smile—my favorite combination.

Kate unbuckles my pants and I lift up to accommodate her as she yanks them off. More slowly, she peels my boxers down and my impatient dick bounces up to greet her.

"And I love your cock." She drives the point home by running her wet tongue up and down it, then swirling around the head.

I look at her beautiful face and grin. "I love my cock in your mouth."

Her lips vibrate against me as she chuckles—and the sensation make my legs tremble. Then she suctions with her lips from base to tip—tauntingly—without actually taking me inside. When I'm on the brink of losing my fucking mind, she opens up and slides my dick into the tight, hot wetness of her mouth.

My head lolls back and I groan.

She swallows me slowly, inch by inch. It's maddening and feels eye-crossingly fantastic at the same time. I can't decide if I want her to suck me hard and fast or to draw out the blissful torture for hours. Maybe days.

When I'm nestled in Kate's throat, she pauses, breathing softly.

And I hiss, "Fuck . . ."

Kate was always skillful at giving head—a real natural. But in these last years, her talents have reached epic proportions. She's a maestro and I'm her well-endowed instrument. She practically trained the gag reflex right out of herself, and she actually enjoys deep throating—and swallowing.

She once told me it made her feel powerful. Watching my face as she works me over. Seeing the signs of pleasure she's controlling—letting me revel in. It's a pretty accurate take on the situation, because at the moment I'm at Kate's complete and total mercy.

And that, kiddies, is the best fucking seat in the house.

She sucks me hard as her head glides up, so just the tip remains between her beautiful lips. She swirls with her tongue again—this time with more pressure, less teasing. Then she bobs up and down quickly—meaning business—all tongue, decadent sloppy wetness, and rough brushes of teeth. Her cheeks hollow out and her hand massages my balls, giving them a gentle, erotic tug.

I moan and curse and chant her name.

I grip her hair and guide her up and down on my dick with just enough force to make her hum in appreciation.

"Yeah, baby, just like that. So fucking good." I gasp.

Kate's lips tighten and her head moves faster.

"Jesus, Kate, I'm gonna come."

My hand clenches and I hold her in place, and every muscle in my body contracts in screaming, unanimous pleasure. My teeth grind and my hips thrust, and with moans of her own, Kate swallows enthusiastically until I have nothing left.

My breathing is harsh as she gifts me with one last flick of her tongue. Then she comes up smiling and climbs onto my lap. And I'm boneless—totally, sublimely relaxed. Screw wine: a blow job is the best way to unwind after a long day at work.

The only thing that would make it better is if I could return the favor.

As I enclose Kate in my arms, I add another tick to the running total of orgasms I owe her. This makes . . . fifteen. And I plan on settling up all in one night—the night Roberta says Kate's good to go. Don't worry—as long I keep her hydrated, there's no physical danger from too many orgasms. I asked.

"I think I'm going to go take that bath you mentioned," she purrs. "Want to join me?"

I run my knuckles along her jaw. "Joining you is just one of the things I'm dying to do right now."

"Things like washing my back?"

I brush my lips against hers. "I want to wash lots of places—every nook and cranny."

Unfortunately, washing her back and rubbing her shoulders are all I'll be able to do tonight. But it'll be enough for now.

I keep her legs wrapped around me as I stand up, bare assed, and walk us to the bathroom.

Having two working parents in the house isn't always perfect—schedule conflicts and work-related stress can get in the way. But it works for us.

Now, where were we again? Before we cut to the gratuitous blow-job scene?

That's right—elbow deep in the massacre that is James's diaper. Try mouth-breathing—it helps with the stench.

"Good God, kid . . . what'd you do last night? Sneak out of the crib and eat a T-bone steak?"

Which brings me to the greatest invention of our time. Nope—it's not the Internet. Or the automobile. It's not female birth control—though that's a good one too. The best innovation of the last century is the Diaper Genie. It's a lifesaver.

I drop the toxic ball into the holy can and quickly close the lid. Then I get him cleaned up with the heated wipes and sprinkle on baby powder. Next I head over to the closet to pick out his clothes. A black, collared shirt, jeans, and Nike sneakers. Clothes make the man—and it works the same way with boys. It's all about first impressions. If you actually *want* your kid getting knocked on his ass in the sandbox? Put him in one of those pansy sweater vests. That'll pretty much guarantee it. James is a cool kid—and I make damn sure he dresses like one.

After I gel James's hair and brush his teeth—with some helpful suggestions on his spitting technique—I carry him to the kitchen airplane style. *Zoom.* And strap him in his high chair so he can't escape.

Next up? Breakfast. You remember how I love cereal, right? That hasn't changed. It's Lucky Charms for me—with extra marshmallows.

But for my son? No Lucky Charms.

Those *Breakfast Club* kids actually knew what they were talking about. And we really do turn into our frigging parents. And phrases like *We'll see* and *Because I said so* just pop into your head and fly out of your mouth. It's disturbing. Like *Exorcist*-possession kind of shit.

Anyway, for James's breakfast? Organic-apple slices and whole-grain Cheerios—without sugar.

I know—it's official—I'm a hypocrite. I can live with that. It's not like his taste buds know what they're missing. And when they do, I'll shove it down his throat anyway. Because it's good for him. If one day he decides to hate me for that? That's okay too.

Because sometimes being a father is hard. And if it's not? You're not doing it right.

I pour some Cheerios onto the tray and back up halfway across the room. "Hey, James, set it up."

He opens his mouth wide and keeps it open. I hold a single Cheerio between my fingers while I bend my knees and bounce my hand as if I were dribbling a basketball. "Three seconds left on the clock, down by one, Evans gets the ball. He fakes left, he drives in, he shoots. . . ."

I toss the Cheerio in a high arc. It lands right in James's mouth.

"He scores! The crowd goes wild!"

James holds both hands over his head. "Core!"

Then I give him a high five. See—told you. Cool, right? I shovel a spoonful of cereal in my mouth and get ready for another shot. Then Kate comes into the kitchen, texting on her phone.

All that worry about losing the baby weight? It was for nothing. Look at her—snug black yoga pants hug narrow hips, a navy Penn State T-shirt shows off her flat stomach and toned arms. Her hair's pulled back into a ponytail, and a touch of shiny, strawberry-flavored lip gloss is her only makeup.

Gorgeous.

Kate still has that simple, low-maintenance kind of beauty. She doesn't have to work at being hot—she just is. I maneuver next to James's high chair and wait for Kate to look up.

Yes, it's deliberate. Children have the power to suck the sex drive out of a relationship like a hungry black hole. So it's important to stoke the flame—keep the coals burning hot. And something about seeing a shirtless guy with a baby turns every woman on.

Trust me—I've been accosted at the beach enough times to know. It's like female frigging Viagra.

It's different for guys. Not that a baby is a negative, necessarily—but seeing a chick with one doesn't automatically make us want to bang her. Because deep, deep down all men are still little boys. We want all your attention on us. It's just how it is.

I feel Kate's eyes on me and I pop a piece of apple into James's mouth. Then I stretch out my arms—flexing the muscles—giving her a good show. Oh, yeah—it's working. She's definitely wet. See how her head tilts and her eyes shine as she looks me up and down? How her lips part and she breathes just a little bit faster?

She's remembering what we just finished doing—and thinking about when we'll get to do it again.

"Mummy!"

Kate's eyes shift to James. Her smile changes—no sexy, more sweet. "Hey, little man."

She comes over and takes an apple slice for herself. "How are my two favorite guys doing?"

"So far, so good." I nod toward the phone in her hand. "What's up there?"

"I'm texting Billy's manager Steven and Alexandra's address. The one he was given is for a pawnshop in the middle of the Bronx. You wouldn't know anything about that, would you?"

My parents are watching all the grandchildren for the weekend. Since Steven and my sister's two trumps our one, the whole gang's meeting at their place and taking a car to the airport together.

I play innocent. "Who me? Nope—I know nothing."

She doesn't look as if she buys it. "He could've missed the car to the airport. Maybe the whole flight."

"Yeah, that would've been a shame."

"Be nice, Drew."

"He's coming, isn't he? I think letting your ex-boyfriend tag along to my bachelor party is above and beyond the call of nice."

Kate motions with her hands as she attempts to defend donkey dump. "You're always complaining about how close I am with him, but maybe if *you* tried a little harder, he wouldn't depend so much on me. And besides, Billy doesn't have a lot of guy friends."

"Which makes perfect sense. He's a pussy—and females tend to flock together."

Kate rolls her eyes.

James decides to join the conversation. "Poosy."

Oh, crap. That's not good.

But still, I start to laugh. How can I not?

Kate frowns at me. "Great."

Most kids speak their first word around the eleven-month mark. Because my son is a genius, his first word came at nine months. And it wasn't *Mama* or *Dada* or anything typical like that.

James's first word was *shit*. Kate was not pleased.

Between you and me, though, we got off easy. It could have been *so* much worse.

She turns to James and admonishes gently, "No, James."

He shakes his head, trying to understand. "No poosy?"

I crack up harder. Now Kate is glaring. She puts her hands on her hips. "Yes—and that's exactly what Daddy's going to be getting if he doesn't stop laughing right now."

James's eyes go wide and he tries to warn me. "No poosy, Daddy."

Now I'm full-out laughing my ass off.

Kate throws her hands up in the air. "Well, that's just perfect! Now he's going to spend the next two days with your parents talking like a foulmouthed little hooligan. What's your mother going to think?"

I sober slightly, still smiling, taking her hand in mine and holding it against my chest. "Considering she's the woman who had to raise the first foulmouthed hooligan? I think she'll have an enormous amount of sympathy for you."

Kate grins. "Which is totally deserved. I swear, between the two of you, I don't know how I keep my sanity."

"It's the sex. If raisins are nature's candy, screwing is its antidepressant. It's the best way to maintain good mental health."

An orgasm a day keeps the psychiatrist away.

Kate crosses her arms doubtfully. "Sure it is. That sounds an awful lot like when I was pregnant and you told me women who performed oral sex more often were less likely to develop preeclampsia."

I point my finger at her. "That was totally true! I read an article about it."

How awesome is *that*? If I wasn't sure before, after that I was certain—God is definitely a guy.

"In what magazine? *Playboy*?"

"*Men's Health.*"

Feeling left out, James tries to get another laugh out of me. "Poosy!"

I ruffle his hair. "Now you're just showing off."

Kate scoops him out of the chair and holds him close. "Are you done with breakfast, baby? Do you want to sing with Mommy?"

He claps his hands.

Most of James's likes and dislikes mirror my own. He hates broccoli. Female sportscasters get on his nerves. And he despises televised figure skating. But he loves Kate's voice.

Oh—and her boobs. See how he bends down to rub his face against them? Reveling in their symmetrical, cushiony softness.

I nudge his shoulder. "Dude, we've been over this—they were loaners. You're cut off now."

Kate breast-fed for the first year. Weaning was hell. Not that I blame the kid—if Kate told me her perfect tits were off-limits? I'd pitch a fucking fit too.

James's little face scrunches up—like Damien from *The Omen*.

He grabs on to Kate's shoulders with both hands and yells, "Mine. Is my mummy!"

I pull her a little closer to my side. "Technically, she belongs to both of us, buddy. We can share. But those?" I point to Kate's breasts. "Those are mine."

He ups the volume. "No. Is mine!"

Sigmund Freud would have a field day in this house.

I shake my head. "I don't think so."

"Is my mummy!"

Getting into a yelling match with a two-year-old is not a good idea. That's a battle that cannot be won.

Kate pushes my chest. "Stop teasing him. And go shower—we're gonna be late."

I kiss her forehead. Then, behind her back, I point to myself and mouth to James, *Mine.*

He blows a raspberry at me. *Smart-ass.*

As I back out of the kitchen, Kate starts to sing. In that soft, flawless voice that still makes me weak in the knees.

And stiff in the crotch.

I know the song—"Jet Plane" by John Denver—but she changes the lyrics to fit the situation.

'Cause we're leavin' on a jet plane
We'll be back on Sunday again
Oh, James, we love you so.

Kate rocks back and forth slowly, and James's deep brown eyes turn to her alone. He looks up at her with complete adoration. Overwhelming worship. Total devotion.

It's the same way I look at her. Every day.

I'm not a big fan of humility. But watching the two of them

like this? It makes me feel humble. Fortunate. Like how Joseph must have felt seeing his wife hold baby Jesus. Just so fucking lucky to get to be a part of something so beautifully sacred.

We're leavin' on a jet plane
We'll be back on Sunday again
Oh, James, we love you so.

I drag my eyes away and head for the shower.

Chapter 3

We get to my sister's place a little after 7:00 A.M. The apartment is a madhouse—the sounds of yelling kids, talking adults, clattering coffee cups, and barking dogs fill the air.

Well . . . one barking dog. His name is Bear—he's a Great Dane. I got him for Mackenzie last Christmas because Applejack the pony didn't exactly work out as I'd planned. Despite some serious begging, pleading, and negotiating, the Bitch wouldn't break down and agree to let the pony I bought Mackenzie for Christmas live with them. Her main reason was the Central Park West Homeowners Association.

If you're not familiar with these types of organizations, I'll fill you in. They're the geriatric version of the gestapo—composed mostly of bitter, wrinkly old bags who lie in wait for someone to do something they don't approve of.

Such as hang a gaudy wreath on the door or play music too loud . . . or convert a bedroom into a barnyard stall.

Instead of trying to buck the system and risk eviction procedures, Steven and Alexandra relocated Applejack to my parents' place upstate—leaving my poor niece without a live-in pet. Which was utterly fucking unacceptable. Hence—Bear.

He's awesome. And big. Sort of like a pony's dwarf cousin.

But he's gentle—great with kids—even though he has no idea how large he actually is. He's always trying to climb into Alexandra's purse or sit on Steven's lap—which can make breathing difficult.

Kate and I walk into the living room with James on my shoulders, and Bear welcomes us with deep woofs and slobbering licks. We greet the parentals, and Kate heads into the kitchen with my mother—rattling off a list of instructions and unloading James's paraphernalia for the overnight stay. I put my son on his feet and he waddles over to the corner where his cousin Thomas is quietly constructing a tower of blocks.

If Mackenzie is my sister Alexandra's twin? Tommy-boy is all Steven. He's a little underweight for his age. But long—lanky. His hair is dark, his eyes are blue and thoughtful. Thomas is easygoing. Laid-back. The perfect yin to my son's Tasmanian-devil-like yang.

With a diabolical giggle, James obliterates Thomas's tower. But he doesn't complain. He just starts building another one. I wrestle with Bear a bit, until my sister walks in with a cup of hot coffee for me.

I take the cup and gesture toward Bear. "How's the house-training going?" Bear has a weak bladder. And though it doesn't detract from his appeal, he's not exactly the sharpest tool in the shed.

"Fantastic—*if* the goal was to turn my nine-thousand-dollar Persian rug into his pissing ground."

I glance at the rug in question. "He's got good taste. That's a fugly rug, Lexi. I'm thinking about pissing on it myself."

"Funny."

I sip my coffee. "I try."

She leads me toward the adjoining dining room. "I talked to the wedding planner last night and finished the seating chart. Take a look."

The wedding.

Okay—most guys would rather have their teeth pulled than have any involvement in the wedding planning. Sorry to break it to you, ladies, but we don't give a shit about colors or centerpieces or the embossing style of the goddamn invitations. If we act as if we do, it's only because we're smart—and we're trying to keep you off our backs.

As long as the bride looks good and those mini hot dogs are served during the cocktail hour? We're there.

So in the beginning, I happily left all the details of the big day to Kate and my sister. But then I started hearing such words as *low-key* and *small, intimate affair* and *nothing too ostentatious*. And I had to step in.

Because when an Olympian wins the gold medal, do they have a *small, intimate affair*?

Of course not.

They throw a fucking ticker-tape parade.

Which is the least of what Kate deserves. Because she did what everyone—including the members of my immediate family—thought impossible. She bagged me. The grand prize—the unattainable—the megamillions jackpot.

That should be celebrated. In a huge way.

Plus, a woman's wedding day is supposed to be special—unforgettable. She only gets one. This is particularly true in Kate's case, because shortly after James was born, we had that whole discussion about what we would do if one of us kicked the bucket early. You've heard of that "*It's a far, far better thing I do*" guy in *A Tale of Two Cities*? The one who sacrificed himself so the woman he loved could go on to live with another man?

Fucking pansy. He deserved to hang. I'm not him.

Sure, I want Kate to be happy—but I want her happy *with me*. Or no one at all. So if I bite the big one before her? She's just gonna have to muddle through on her own.

Single.

Celibate.

Because if she hooks up with another guy? Has my son calling some loser Daddy?

I'll haunt her. Forever. Like, *The Grudge* style.

You think that's awful, don't you? Selfish, possessive, egotistical?

And this surprises you why?

Anyway—back to the wedding. Once I took over the reins, things got jacked up a whole lot of notches—no expense spared, no detail overlooked. Alexandra and I work great together. Her hyperactive planning and organizational skills coupled with my micromanaging and determination for the perfect day have made a stupendous combination. We also have the assistance of Lauren Laforet, the most sought-after wedding planner in the city, making sure all our big plans become a reality.

Prince William and Kate can kiss my ass. *Amateurs.* We've got this wedding-of-the-century thing in the bag.

On the dining-room table sits a model of the Four Seasons ballroom, with dozens of miniature tables and hundreds of name-labeled chairs perfectly arranged.

I'm impressed. "This is amazing."

She pushes a strand of blond hair behind her ear, contemplating her handiwork. "I know."

I notice one table doesn't look right. I'm about to comment, but a commotion in the living room signals a new arrival. I move to the doorway to see who's here.

"Woof! Wooof!"

It's Brangelina. Otherwise known as Matthew and Delores. Curious about the nickname? You'll see.

"Get off me, beast!"

Bear has a real hard-on for Dee-Dee. Literally. He tries to violate her every chance he gets. Maybe he's just horny. Maybe he likes how her ass smells. Maybe he instinctually senses that she's a freak who'd be into bestiality—I don't know. Whatever the reason?

Funniest fucking thing ever.

"Matthew, help! He's licking me! He's drooling on me!"

"Down, Bear!"

Steven appears and drags the hot and bothered hound out of the room. Dee-Dee adjusts her outfit—a green silk halter jumpsuit, with a royal-blue poncholike cape and silver stiletto heels. Reminds me of a strawberry-blond, hazel-eyed peacock.

Matthew pounds me warmly on the arm. "Hey, man."

"Hey."

Then Mackenzie walks into the room. She's taller than the last time you saw her—she'll most likely get to five feet ten by the time she's done growing. Her hair's still long and blond with a slight curl; she's wearing blue jeans, Converse sneakers, and a pink Yankees jersey. She's a month shy of nine now—in this day and age, that's practically a preteen.

Mackenzie is a masterpiece—and I take full credit.

She's polite, brilliant, feminine—but not in a screechy afraid-of-spiders way. She watches sports—not to get the attention of some little prick, but because she knows what a two-point conversion and a technical foul are. She paints her nails and plays guitar. She's confident but kind. Best of all, she takes shit from no one. Yeah—that's all me.

Even though I have my own son now, she was the first. The only girl. A piece of my heart will always, always belong to her.

"Hey, sweetheart."

She jumps up and throws herself into my arms. I spin her around.

"Hi, Uncle Drew! I didn't know you were here."

"Just got here. I like your shirt."

Then, from down the hall, I hear Steven and Alexandra going at it. And not in a good way.

"I told you to put him in his crate!"

"I was going to but—"

"*Going to* isn't doing! I should've just done it myself—like everything else around here."

"Can you give the martyr complex a rest, please?"

They've been like this lately. Tense. Strained. We've all noticed. It happens—live with someone long enough, they're bound to get on your fucking nerves. My sister's nag-athons don't exactly make it easy. But Steven's always known what she's like, and he worshipped her anyway.

Until now.

It's his tone that bothers me the most. He sounds tired. Worn-out. Fed up.

Mackenzie gazes at the floor.

I grasp her chin and tilt her face up. "How's it been around here?"

She sighs. "Dramatic."

I glance down the hall. "Yeah, I'm sensing that."

"That's parents for you." She shrugs. "Can't live with 'em, but emancipation is a costly and complicated process."

I chuckle. "You know my door's always open, right? There's a spare room with your name on it."

She glances at Thomas. "But that would leave Thomas holding down the fort. He's just a little kid."

"And what are you?"

Blue eyes stare up at me—wise beyond their years. "I'm the big sister."

I lean over and kiss her forehead. Then I whisper, "This weekend will be good for them, I promise. Like a mini vacation. And I'll talk to them—knock their heads together."

She gives me a soft smile, as if she appreciates my effort but doesn't quite believe it'll do any good. "Okay, Uncle Drew."

Matthew walks over, oblivious of everything but Mackenzie. "There's my girl!"

She looks back at him and the smile free-falls from her face. She raises her nose and folds her arms. Did you feel the temperature drop? That'd be from my niece's cold shoulder.

"Mr. Fisher, how nice to see you again. You're looking well."

Matthew groans and drops to his knees. Even though he's over six foot, with a boxer's frame, he looks almost diminutive when faced with my niece's displeasure. "Mackenzie, you're killing me, baby."

"I'm sure I don't know what you mean."

He pushes a frustrated hand through his light brown hair. "Are you ever going to forgive me?"

"Forgive you? For what? For depriving me of growing up with female companionship? For leaving me wallowing in a forest of penises? Is that what I should forgive you for, Mr. Fisher?"

Having babies is contagious—like mono. Once a friend or a relative has one, everyone wants one just like it. At Thanksgiving dinner, the year after James was born, Matthew and Dee-Dee announced that they were having a baby. That they were *adopting* a baby.

Brangelina? Get it now?

After they proclaimed their intentions, everyone was happy for them.

Well . . . almost everyone:

"What do you mean, you're adopting a baby?" asks Frank Fisher, as he sits at the dining-room table of my parents' country house on Thanksgiving Day.

Still holding his wife's hand, Matthew faces his father. "What do you mean, what do I mean? We're adopting a little boy! The paperwork is filed, and we're waiting on the final approval, but the agency says that's just a formality. Dee and I have passed all the big hurdles. He's almost two months old—he's healthy and gorgeous." Matthew turns to Estelle. "I can't wait for you to see him, Mom."

Estelle beams back at her son with budding tears of joy. But Frank asks, "Is something wrong with your wife? Is she barren?"

Matthew's smile falters. Before he can answer, Delores retorts, "No, Frank, I'm not barren. This is something Matthew and I have talked about doing since we were married."

Frank wipes his mouth with his cloth napkin, tosses it down on his plate, and pushes back from the table. The air shifts—like a summer afternoon when the sun is shining, but the wind picks up and you can feel the storm that's about to burst over your head.

"Why the hell would you want to raise a child that isn't yours, Matthew?"

My best friend frowns. "Because he will *be ours."*

"No," Frank argues, "that's my point—he won't be. You have no idea where this kid comes from, what kind of garbage his real parents are. He could grow up to have mental problems, health issues—and you'll be stuck dealing with that for the rest of your life."

Although part of me suspects my father agrees with him, he still tries to get Frank to lighten up. "That's a defeatist view, Frank. Cases like that are rare when you look at the millions of children who are adopted each year."

By this time I'm on my feet, positioning myself closer to Matthew. Because I suspect this pot is about to boil the fuck over. In looks, Matthew resembles his father, but in personality he takes more after Estelle. Not much bothers him—he has a long fuse. But when he blows? It's like the finale at the Macy's fireworks extravaganza.

Then Frank does the one thing that's sure to light Matthew's fuse: he lays into Dee-Dee. "This is your doing, isn't it? You and your liberal, new age bullshit!"

"Frank, please," Estelle pleads softly.

"You're too self-centered to take time from your career to fulfill your duties as a wife."

"My duties?" Delores shouts from behind Matthew. "What year are you living in, Frank?"

"Doesn't matter the year—a woman is a woman, and a mother is a mother. Unless she physically can't, a good woman gives her husband children. If you're not up to the task, young lady, then my son would be smart to replace you with a woman who is."

Hello, shit. Meet fan.

Matthew steps forward, the urge to put his father right through my mother's professionally painted mural wall written all over his face. "Don't ever *fucking talk to her like that again!"*

I grab Matthew's shoulder, holding him back. "C'mon, buddy, let's take a walk outside."

He shrugs me off.

In a lifeless voice Delores says, "I'd like to go home now. Matthew, can we please go?"

He looks over his shoulder at her crestfallen face, and even though none of this is his fault, remorse is in his eyes. "Yeah, yeah, we're leaving."

He turns to me—because Matthew and Delores drove up with me, Kate, and James in our new Escalade.

I nod. "Kate—get the baby's stuff. I'll get our coats."

Looking as if she wants to plunge her stiletto into Dee's father-in-law's forehead, Kate agrees. She brings Delores with her to gather our son and his gear. Estelle wrings her hands and weeps silently.

Frank just won't let it frigging go. "When this blows up in your face, Matthew, don't come crying to me."

Matthew replies with a mixture of anger and hurt, "Don't worry—I would never fucking consider it." He glances at his mother. "Sorry, Mom." Then he walks out of the room and I'm right behind him.

The ride home is quiet. James falls asleep before we hit the highway. My friend and his wife hold hands in the backseat, whispering apologies and reassurances to each other.

Delores cries.

I don't like it. It makes her seem so . . . human.

I offer my take on the situation. "I think we can all agree that sucked sweaty balls. But Frank's not going to be a dick about it forever. He was blindsided—and he's worried about you." I make eye contact with my best friend in the review mirror. "Remember when you bought the Ducati?"

Even though Matthew was twenty-two at the time, the way Frank blew a gasket when he saw his son's motorcycle, you would've thought he was sixteen and taking out a Lamborghini for a joyride. The first time Matthew rode it to the office, Frank bribed the maintenance guys to remove one of the fucking tires.

Even though Frank went about it the wrong way, it stemmed from his concern for his son. Trying to protect him—desperately not wanting to see him become roadkill. This situation isn't any different.

"I remember," Matthew begrudgingly admits.

"It's the same thing. He'll get over it."

Matthew's jaw clenches. "Well, maybe I fucking won't. He insulted my wife. And this isn't a motorcycle, Drew. This is my kid."

I sigh, 'cause I knew he was going to say that. "I know. But I bet once my parents and Lexi get through guilt-tripping him, he'll be kissing your ass come Monday. Frank's going to see the error of his ways and apologize. To you too, Dee. Just watch."

Only . . . he didn't.

Matthew and Frank didn't speak to each other for two whole weeks.

Then adoption day came.

They flew to Transylvania or one of those small Eastern Bloc countries, and they came back with a beautiful baby boy. The weird thing is, he actually looks like them—bright hazel eyes and brown hair with natural-blond highlights.

Estelle broke the standoff. She threatened to leave the stubborn bastard if he didn't tell Matthew and Dee how sorry he was—how wrong he had been.

The day after they brought the baby home, they threw a small family party so everyone could meet the new addition. I watched Frank from the second he walked into Matthew's apartment.

Proud. Distant. Hard.

Until he saw his son, holding his own son.

And all of his proud ideals about how things should be just kind of melted away.

The Discovery Channel has a show about gorillas. At first, male gorillas feel threatened by their offspring. They don't understand them, sort of ignore them, or bang their chests whenever they're around. But then, after a couple days, they get used to them. And God fucking help anyone who tries to mess with them.

It was a lot like that.

After that first visit, from the moment Frank held the baby, he decided that this was his grandson in every way. And he'd happily beat the crap out of anyone who said otherwise.

It's been smooth sailing ever since.

Now, back to Matthew's groveling.

Delores comes to his rescue and kneels down in front of Mackenzie. "I understand why you're upset, Mackenzie. I didn't have any girl cousins, either."

Mackenzie throws her arms up in the air. "I just don't get it! You got to *pick* your baby! It wasn't like with Aunt Kate and Mommy, where we just had to take what we got. Why couldn't you have picked a girl?"

Dee smiles softly. "We didn't pick Rain, sweetie. He picked us. And even though he didn't grow in my body, he grew in my heart. He was supposed to be our son—there really was no choice."

Mackenzie breathes deep. "Well, the next time you decide to grow a baby, could you please tell your heart we need another girl around here?"

Matthew pulls her in for a hug and squeezes her tight. "I'll do my best."

Personally, I'm relieved they got a boy. You know that saying "It takes a village to raise a child"? That's all wrong. It takes a village to raise a *girl.* Pick a headline—any headline. Lindsay Lohan, Britney Spears, Miley Cyrus—it's not their fault they're train wrecks. It's because they didn't have people in their lives who cared enough about them to teach them. Prepare them for what is still mostly a man's world.

Boys are easy. Keep the fridge stocked, smack them around once in a while, discourage them from jumping off the roof into the swimming pool, make sure they use soap when they shower. That's pretty much it.

Girls are a whole other animal. You have to worry about low self-esteem and poor self-image, eating disorders, cutting, drug abuse, sluttiness, catty mean-girl attitudes, and the horde of adolescent bastards who are just dying to get their dicks wet and won't give a damn if they leave a broken heart, pregnancy, or an STD in their wake.

Even though Mackenzie is coming along nicely, once puberty hits, all bets are off. The fewer distractions I have when those days come, the better.

As Matthew and Delores get up off the floor, I ask, "Where is Michael, anyway? With Helga?"

Unlike Kate and me, Matthew and Dee had no issues about hiring a nanny. And Delores may be crazy, but she's not stupid—no way she was gonna have some sexy, young au pair rocking her cradle. Helga's a professional Russian nanny. She's suspicious and distrustful of anyone not related to Michael—and sometimes even of those who are. She bears a strong resemblance to Brutus from the *Popeye* cartoons. She's got a femstache and a permanent scowl, and she could probably kick my ass with one hand tied behind her back.

I like her.

Because she thinks the sun rises and sets with my nephew. She calls him her babushka, and it's easy to see that she'd lie, cheat, steal, or kill for him. That makes her okay in my book.

Mackenzie giggles. "Uncle Drew, Rain's name isn't Michael, it's Rain."

Dee-Dee's eyes turn sharp as they regard me. "Uncle Drew knows his name, Mackenzie. He's just being a jerk."

I stare Dee-Dee down, not giving an inch. "Rain isn't a name. It's a meteorological event. Every child deserves a normal name. He'll always be Michael to me."

I'm working on having his birth certificate changed. A little forgery never hurt anyone. Christ, what kind of uncle would I be if I let the kid go through life with a fucking name like Rain? As if the chips weren't already stacked against him with a crazy woman for a mother.

"You're an ass."

"It's not his fault his mother's a wack job and his father's a victim of reverse spousal abuse."

Matthew adds his pathetic two cents: "I like the name Rain."

So sad.

I sneer, "No, you don't." I point to my temple. "That's the brainwashing talking. She's got you under her evil spell. You've been twat-notized by the golden watch between Dee's legs."

If I slap him hard enough, think he'll snap out of it?

Delores doesn't take it lying down. "Brainwashed? Look who's talking. James is *your* golden watch. I swear sometimes that's the only thing keeping Kate with you."

A few years ago that comment would have bothered me. Not anymore. "Please. We all know it's my dick that's keeping her with me. And that's not going anywhere anytime soon, so I'm really not worried."

Before Dee can retaliate, the front door slams open with a bang, and the blur of an eight-year-old, light-haired boy comes barreling through the living room. He gives my sister a crooked grin. "Hi, Mrs. R."

Alexandra smiles. "Hi, Johnny." Then she turns toward our parents. "Mom, Dad, you remember Johnny Fitzgerald from downstairs? He's kindly offered his services this weekend to help keep the little ones entertained."

Johnny Fitzgerald. Sound familiar? Think back, way back.

I'll give you a minute to flex the old memory.

*
*
*
*
*
*
*
*
*
*
*
*
*
*
*
*
*
*
*
*
*
*
*
*
*
*
*
*

Remember the foolish, misguided preschooler who told Mackenzie that penises were better than baginas, a lifetime ago? Yep—*that* Johnny Fitzgerald.

He lives one floor down. Ever since preschool, he and Mackenzie have been connected at the hip. His dad's an old-money asshole—his mom's a functioning alcoholic. Alexandra has him over as often as possible so he can gain exposure to a normal family unit.

Mackenzie pokes her finger at Johnny. "You can help—but you have to do what I say. *I'm* in charge."

I throw a smirk my sister's way. "Boy, does that sound familiar."

On cue, James squawks from the corner. "Mine! Is mine!"

Alexandra lifts an eyebrow. "So does that. Must be genetic."

Then Mackenzie and Johnny's newest battle of the sexes begins. "Hold on a second, Kenzie," he says. "I should be in charge. I'm a boy and they're boys."

"So?"

"So, I can show them how to do things you can't."

My niece's hands fall to her hips, imitating my sister's stance perfectly. Talk about genetics. "Like what?"

"I can show them to throw a baseball."

"So can I."

"I can play cars with them."

Mackenzie scoffs, "So can I."

Johnny goes in for the kill. "I can show them how to pee standing up."

There's a heavy pause. Mackenzie frowns.

Johnny starts to think he's won. *So young, so dumb.*

Until Mackenzie smiles. Triumphantly. "They wear diapers—they don't use the toilet yet."

Johnny lowers his head in submission. *Might as well get used to it now, kid.* "Okay—you can be in charge."

Mackenzie smiles wider. Then she taps her fingers together, not unlike Mr. Burns from *The Simpsons*. "Excellent."

Chapter 4

Ten minutes later, Jack O'Shay shows up. He's wearing a smart, light blue button-down and casual slacks. His red hair is cut short and gelled within an inch of its life. Jack's the last of my single friends. The lone wolf. A desperado. He's still living the life I always thought I'd have. Spontaneous. Irresponsible. Uninhibited. He takes great pleasure in ragging on us about all the great nights—and wild snatch—we're missing out on.

Not going to lie; I get a kick out of his stories—because I remember how much fun a random hookup can be. But I wouldn't trade places with him in a million years. The grass doesn't get any greener then Kate Brooks.

We're all gathered in the kitchen now, where my mom and sister have laid out a continental breakfast. Jack chews on a fresh-baked croissant and chats with my mother. "You're looking lovely as always, Mrs. Evans."

She giggles like a cheerleader talking to the star quarterback. *Ewww.* "Thank you, Jack. That's sweet of you to say."

"Just being honest. Now tell me—how often do you get mistaken for the nanny when you're out with these little guys? 'Cause there's no way anyone would believe you're a grandma."

It sounds like he's coming on to my mom, but he's not. When you're a player, this is just how you talk—to *all* women. Remember that the next time some hotshot is dazzling you with his verbal diarrhea. You're not special—he doesn't mean it. It's just his nature.

My father doesn't seem to appreciate this fact, however. See how he moves closer to my mom? How he scowls in Jack's direction? "Don't talk to my wife, O'Shay."

Jack instantly sobers and steps back. "Yes, sir."

"Don't look at her, either."

"No, sir."

My old man may be getting on in years, but he still knows he's at the top of the food chain. The last thing Jack wants is to get chewed up and spit out. He segues the conversation toward something safer.

"So, Mr. Evans, you're not coming with us this weekend?"

My dad shakes his head, and his tone is filled with regret. And longing. "No, not this time. Though I wish I could go with you boys. So much."

My mother's head whips around. "Oh, really, John?"

He coughs. And clears his throat. "Yes . . . well . . . you know . . . for the sports betting. You know how I enjoy sports betting, Anne. And we don't have that . . . here . . . in New York."

Nice save, Pops. Nice save.

My mother nods skeptically. "Uh-huh."

At which point the old man deflects my mother's negative attention toward a more obvious target. Which would be me, of course.

"You boys have fun this weekend, but be safe. Remember the last time we were in Vegas, Andrew? Let's not have a repeat."

When I was seventeen, my father had business in Vegas. He and my mother thought it would just be a *wonderful* idea to make a family trip out of it. But I was *seventeen*. A time in a guy's life when he doesn't even want to admit that he knows his family—let alone spend time with them. So, while my parents, Alexandra, and Steven were off visiting the Hoover Dam, I was forced to occupy myself with other . . . activities.

"I've said it a thousand times, Dad—I didn't know she was the ambassador's daughter." They should make them wear dog tags or tattoos on their foreheads or something. I roll my eyes and say to no one in particular, "One international incident and they never let you forget it."

Kate appears at my side. Her gorgeous face is contemplative, digesting what she has just heard. "Do I want to know?"

Don't even have to think about this one. "It's probably best if you don't."

She nods. "Good enough for me."

Next to arrive is Erin Burrows. She's still my secretary, but in the last two years she's become much more. At times my schedule is so packed, Kate talks to Erin more than she talks to me. At other times, when clients want both members of the dynamic duo at the conference table, Erin takes over James duty. Even though she's technically an employee, Erin calls it like it is. In other words, she's a friend. One of the gang. And cool to hang out with. So when this soiree was slapped together, Kate and I couldn't imagine not inviting her to come along.

After greeting James, Erin joins the rest of us near the kitchen table. She's changed her hair. It's shorter, straight, and has tasteful honey-colored streaks.

Kate approves. “Your hair looks great, Erin.”

She fingers her tresses. “Thanks. I had it done yesterday. I’m pulling out all the stops—this is my weekend to meet Mr. Right. New York men are hopelessly defective. I think Nevada will offer more suitable options.”

Erin dates a lot, but as far as I know, she’s never been in a serious relationship. Las Vegas isn’t exactly the smartest place to find a stellar boyfriend, however. Might as well try your luck at AA or Gamblers Anonymous.

Sex-addict meetings are always a safe bet.

Steven wanders over. “Take my advice, Erin—stay single. Life is less complicated that way.”

Alexandra flinches. Even though he’s one of my oldest, dearest friends, I have the urge to reach into his mouth and rip out his tongue. That’s not wrong, is it?

I let it go. For now.

Matthew offers sagely, “Keep your head up, Erin—it’ll happen. When the time is right, when you least expect it.”

“Yeah—I’m staying optimistic. You have to kiss a lot of frogs before you find a prince.”

Alexandra responds, “They’re all frogs, Erin. Just try and find one with the least amount of warts.”

I elbow Jack. “If we’re talking about the genital variety, you should talk to O’Shay. You’re kind of the in-house expert on those, right man?”

He flips me the bird.

Then the last member of our traveling circus arrives. Care to hazard a guess?

“Yo, party people in the house! Who’s ready to rock?!”

Yep—it’s the douche bag. For Kate’s sake, I try not to hate him as much as I used to—but some things just can’t be helped.

It's like when you have the tail end of a cold and one loogie hangs on to back of your throat. You cough, you hawk, but no matter what you do, you just can't fucking get rid of it.

That's Billy Warren. My personal, annoying ball of phlegm.

Kate and Dee-Dee squeal and hug the dumbass.

He hugs them back. "I've missed you guys."

Kate says, "But you didn't have to fly all the way out here. You could have just met us in Vegas."

"And miss the preparty? No way."

I was hoping his plane would get hijacked by bloodthirsty terrorists. The kind that like to cut off body parts and FedEx them back to the family, one by one. *Oh, well.* There's always the return flight. It's important to stay positive about these things.

His attention turns toward me. His eyes look me up and down stiffly. "Evans."

I raise my chin. "Warren."

He turns around and zeroes in on James. Warren scoops him up and exclaims, "What are you feeding this kid, Kate? He's so much bigger than the last time I saw him."

Yeah. Shocking. 'Cause babies don't usually grow or anything. *Moron.*

"I brought you presents, tadpole. A shiny, noisy set of drums. You're gonna freak when you see it."

James giggles. To the casual observer, it might seem that my son is actually fond of the fuckface. But I know better. Animals can sense when a person's a few cards shy of a full deck. When they're on the lower end of the bell curve. Kids can do that too. James doesn't like Warren—he pities him. Because he knows that, even at two years old, he's smarter than Jackass can ever hope to be.

As the small talk builds to a crescendo, Kate and I look over the seating chart one more time. I put my arm around her just because she's mine. Her eyes are soft and her voice is velvet as she sighs, "Seven more days. About this time next week, I'll be putting my dress on."

It's the one thing that's been kept confidential. Strictly off-limits. "Can't I have a hint? Will there be cleavage? Is it satin? Lace?" I wiggle my eyebrows. "Latex?"

She shakes her head.

"Just tell me you didn't pick some old-fashioned, frilly getup that makes you look like a yeti."

She chuckles. "I'll never tell. But . . . feel free to try and torture the information out of me. By any means necessary."

Several ideas come to mind. Each with the potential of earning me a front-row seat in hell. Possibly a jail cell. "God, I love the way you think."

My sister's voice drags me from my sinful musings. "Oh—I've been meaning to tell you two—we have a problem with table forty-five. A guest hasn't responded yet."

She picks up her trusty clipboard. "He's . . . Brandon Mitchell . . . Delores's stepbrother. He may or may not be bringing a plus one."

Delores's mother got married last summer to some cop from their hometown. It figures that only a man professionally trained in firearms and self-defense would be brave enough to tie the knot with Amelia Warren.

I turn on Delores. "Again with your fucking family. What is it with you people? You're like King Midas in reverse—everything you touch turns to shit."

She argues, "Brandon is not my family."

For once my sister and I are on the same page. She waves her finger in Dee-Dee's face. "Oh, yes, he is. His father married your mother—that makes him yours. If we have to claim Great-Aunt Clara, you have to own up to this Mitchell clown."

Great-Aunt Clara is my grandmother's stepsister, on my mother's side. She's like a thousand years old. The kind of relative we only wheel out of the nursing home once or twice a year for big events. Clara loves to dance, and even for an ancient she can move pretty well.

The things is—since she was born a century ago, when women couldn't vote or show ankle skin—Clara's a big fan of women's liberation. So she refuses to wear a bra.

Ever.

And her breasts are massively huge. Heavy—like dry-cement-stuffed balloons. They should be classified as deadly weapons.

At James's christening? Clara was getting down on the dance floor to the latest Rihanna song. She lifts her arms, spins around . . . and nails my best client's teenage son in the head with her left tit.

The kid was out cold for ten minutes. Thankfully, his parents chose not to sue.

Kate steps between us, hands up, into the line of fire. "Okay, everyone, let's just all take a step back. Dee, call your mom and have her lean on Brandon."

Delores does as she's told. But I go on, "Yeah—lean on him hard. Or he'll be eating dinner in the parking lot with the valets."

Kate's hand snakes around my back, tracing soothing lines under my T-shirt. "Relax, Drew. It's not that big a deal."

Her touch is soft—skin on skin. It feels like a double dose of Valium: instantly calming. My voice holds considerably less heat as I tell her, "This day is going to be goddamn magical. No way I'm letting an honorary Warren mess with it—even if it's just the seating arrangement."

She turns into me, and her arms climb up around my neck. "Are you going to show up at the church?"

I tilt my head back so I can look in her eyes. "Wild lions couldn't keep me away."

"And . . . at some point . . . will we become husband and wife?"

"That's the plan."

She reaches up on her toes and brushes her lips with mine. Once. Twice. "Then it'll be perfect."

Dee-Dee closes her cell and announces, "My mother says Brandon's coming, but he's not bringing a date."

Alexandra amends her list and removes the question-mark chair from the model. Then she beams. "There. Crisis averted. I just need to adjust the number of favors and we're good to go."

Dee's eyes go wide. "Oh, I almost forgot!" She rummages around in her shiny metallic shoulder bag, then raises her arms in victory. "Party favors!"

Fisted in Delores's hands are a dozen lollipops. Each about ten inches long.

In the shape of a dick.

She hands a few to my mother. "Here you go, Anne. Just because you're not partaking in the festivities doesn't mean you can't enjoy a treat." Then she adds with a wink, "Vanilla and chocolate. Yum."

My mother turns the confection around with a mischievous smile and playful glint in her eyes. Then she puts it on the counter. "Thank you, Dee-Dee. I'll save these for after dinner."

My father grins. Broadly.

Great. Now I'm stuck with the image of my sweet, saintly mother sucking down a cock-pop while my old man watches. There's an excellent chance I'll never get a boner again.

Fucking Delores.

Okay, the boner thing is an exaggeration, but still—do you see why I can't stand her? Her and her whole demon family tree. My best friend couldn't marry a normal girl, could he? No—he had to fall for the Bride of Chucky incarnate.

The phone rings. It's the doorman letting us know the limo's here. Everyone files out the door as my parents spread around the hugs and well-wishing.

I snatch James back from Warren for a final farewell.

We're lucky—James is not one of those clingy, whiny little bastards who lose their mind when Mommy walks out the door. Even so—good-byes are never fun.

Kate kisses his cheek and pushes his hair back from his eyes. "We love you, baby. We'll be home soon."

I kiss his head. Then I ask the stupidest question ever. "Are you gonna be good for Grandma and Pop?"

He looks at me sideways. And grins. "No."

I shrug toward Kate. "Well, at least he's honest."

Chapter 5

I'm not a big fan of air travel. For several reasons. First, there's the pilot. You can never be sure he knows what the hell he's doing. Maybe he got his license from a Cracker Jack box. Maybe his daddy made a generous donation to his flight school.

If I want to put my life in jeopardy? I'll ask my sister if she's gained weight.

Then there's the charade of it. No matter how many people those security agents feel up, no matter how many bags those former McDonald's employees search? If somebody really wants to do some damage? Eventually, he will. The airlines should be up-front about it. Like those SWIM AT YOUR OWN RISK signs at the beach. When the desk agent hands you the boarding pass, he or she should say, "Hold on, pray your ass doesn't get blown up, have a nice flight."

Would that really be so bad?

Finally, there's the doom-and-gloom certainty that if something—even accidentally—does go wrong? You're toast. I know what the statistics say—that you're more likely to get into a car accident, blah, blah, blah. But here's the thing—lots of people who've had auto collisions have walked away without a scratch. Now tell me how many people you know who've gotten out of a plane wreck unscathed?

Exactly.

Still—I don't let those worries interfere with my life. They don't get in the way. At all. Because fear doesn't make a coward—actions do. I'm a lot of things, but a chickenshit isn't one of them. And I have to admit, even though it's not my favorite thing to do, there used to be benefits to flying.

Meaning the veritable smorgasbord of available women that can be found in airports and planes. There's the oh-so-lonely housewife, the overworked businesswoman, the carefree graduate student looking to let loose . . . the flight attendant.

In recent years, quality control on that last one has gone majorly downhill. Once upon a time, sex appeal was in the job description. That's no longer the case. But I find the airlines tend to schedule at least one screwable female on every flight. Back in my free-man days, they were the easiest pickings. Always so eager to be of service.

One time, on a business trip to Singapore, three stunning flight attendants were ready, willing, and able to show me the all sights worth seeing—inside their hotel room. We had quite the layover. That's what I call some friendly skies.

Speaking of which, one's headed our way now. She's attractive—slim, tall, long dark hair pulled back at the sides, and deep blue eyes with an exotic slant. Her hands are manicured—delicate—the perfect size for a decent jerking-off.

Yes—guys notice things like that.

"I'm sorry, sir, you'll have to keep your seat belt buckled until the captain turns the sign off."

I look down at the belt in question, then back up. "Right.

'Cause if we nose-dive from twenty thousand feet, this little piece of fabric is gonna stand between me and certain death?"

Like I said—hypocrites.

She laughs. And the yellow seat-belt sign goes out with a ding.

I grin. "Guess he heard me."

Full, pink lips smile. "Guess so."

Blue eyes glance around the first-class cabin. "A little birdie told me you're all headed to Vegas for a prewedding party—and you're the groom."

"That I am."

She hands me a mimosa. "Congratulations."

"Thanks."

She hands Kate a glass as well, then her attention reverts back to me. "So . . . where are you staying?"

I take a sip of the orange concoction. "The Bellagio."

"Nice." She leans over a little—close enough that I can smell her cheap, too-sweet perfume—and drops the bomb. "I'm off the clock once we land in Nevada. I'm staying with friends. . . . Maybe we'll stop by the Bellagio casino tonight? You look like you'd be in the high rollers' section?"

My friends and I aren't flashy about our money—most people who have it aren't. But the signs are there if you know what you're looking for—quality luggage, Rolex watches, classic but expensive brand clothing.

And yes—this chick just stepped over the line. Her words sounded like a proposition, because they were. Which is pretty fucking disrespectful, considering my fiancée is within earshot.

But I'm not surprised. Even though men are supposed to be the bold pursuers? Women can be so much worse. They're brazen. Shameless. They'll stab each other in the back faster than Jason freaking Voorhees.

Just ask Steven. When he and Alexandra were dating? Practically every one of her so-called friends offered to climb on his face and take it for a test ride. Because they were petty. Jealous. Because they wanted what Alexandra had.

Some guys, such as Jack, would welcome crap like this with open arms, always wanting to keep their options open. But not me—not anymore. I play it gracious but firm. Reverently, I pick up Kate's hand and kiss her knuckles, making sure the ring is in sight. "We're going to be pretty busy tonight. Thanks anyway."

She backs off with an offended shrug. "Suit yourself."

It's not the first time this has happened, and it probably won't be the last. Kate handles it well, even though deep down I know it bugs the shit out of her.

I'm not above using that to my advantage, of course. See that devil on my shoulder? Yeah—he's ready to get busy. Watch.

I lean toward Kate. "So . . . you're just going to let her get away with that?"

She continues to stare at her magazine, turning the pages harshly. "Get away with what?"

"With that Hail Mary pass she just threw. Trying to eat off your plate. If a guy came on to you like that in front of me? He'd be eating sidewalk."

"I'm not a teenager, Drew. My days of fighting over a boy are over."

What I wouldn't give to have seen those days. With Jell-O on top.

"I'm not saying you should yank her hair out or rip each other's clothes off"—I chuckle—"though that would be *awesome*. I just think you should teach her a lesson. Show her who I belong to."

Kate closes the magazine, shaking her head slightly. Her eyes are shiny with amusement. "I know what you're doing."

"What am I doing?"

"You're just trying to get me to have sex with you in the bathroom."

Busted. "A blow job will work too. You're really good at those."

She reopens the magazine. "Flattery will get you nowhere, Evans. Least of all into my pants."

I whine, "Why not?"

"Because all of our friends are here."

"So what?"

"So they'll hear us."

I lie, "No, they won't."

"They might."

"I'll stuff your panties in your mouth—they won't hear a thing."

She snorts. And stays strong. "Sounds romantic. Still . . . not happening."

It's *so* happening. But I admit—this banter? The sexual tension? Having to work for it once in a while? It's still fun. Exciting. It keeps my skills razor sharp.

Knowing I'll eventually get my way? That helps too.

I try a different tactic. Guilt. "It's tradition, Kate. Like tapping the mascot symbol when you exit the locker room before a football game. It's bad luck to break tradition—something terrible could happen. How will you feel if this plane crashes and burns, all because you didn't want to give it up?"

"I think I'll take my chances."

I look forward and sigh. This is a five-hour flight. There's no way Kate can hold out that long. Because, when you know how to strum a guitar the right way? That sucker plays.

I give it a few minutes, until her guard is down. Then I turn sideways in my seat. And start off slow. Subtle. One hand on her thigh, drawing leisurely circles. Eventually my other hand joins in, stroking her arm, then her shoulder—relaxing her. Overwhelming her senses.

Notice, she's not pushing me away. Because even though one set of lips is saying no? The other set is always up for a good time.

I lean over and my mouth lightly caresses her cheek, moving gently across her jawline to her neck. My hand creeps down and covers one breast—squeezing and rubbing. Sliding and teasing.

Kate's breathing picks up. The magazine falls from her hands. She half warns, "Drew . . ."

I whisper in her ear, "Just kiss me. That's all I want, baby. Just one kiss."

These are the famous last words spoken by teenage boys everywhere, in the backseat of their parents' car. If there are any young females out there? Be warned—it's never just one kiss. They don't call it stealing bases for nothing. Before you know it, he'll be rounding second, sliding into third, and a home run is just inches away.

Kate presses her mouth to mine—lets me seduce her with my tongue. *So warm. So wet.*

So nice.

Hot, hard, real desire uncoils low in my gut, and my pants tighten predictably. I turn my attention to her earlobe—sucking and biting. Then I whisper tender, dirty, need-filled words that you don't get to hear. About how much I want her, how beautiful she is, about all the things I want to do to her, and the detailed positions I want to do them in.

Kate's hips move upward, searching for friction against the fingers that are now firmly stationed between her legs. When she's primed and panting—right where I want her—I retract my hands. And look into her eyes. "Let's finish this in the other room."

Kate bites her bottom lip. Her slightly dazed eyes dart left to right, making sure there are no witnesses. She's just about to cave . . .

Until a foreign body plops down between us—half on both our laps. My eyes are covered with strawberry-blond hair. And the taste of hair spray fills my mouth.

God damn it.

"Hope you got a good night's sleep last night, Katie. For what I have planned, you're going to need lots of energy."

Delores. As if there were any doubt.

She wiggles her ass off my thigh, forcing Kate and me to move over so she can squeeze in between us.

Kate recovers quickly. "Yep . . . um . . . you know me. I'm all about being well rested."

My body crackles with unspent carnal energy. It makes me cranky. "Do you frigging mind? We were in the middle of something."

Dee-Dee turns toward me with knowing disdain clear on her face. "Nope, don't mind at all." She shoos me away with her hand. "You can amscray—Kate and I have some catching up to do."

"I don't think so."

"Hello? This is a bachelorette party—and it starts now. You're not invited. Go compare peckers with the boys, talk about the massive dump you took last night—or whatever it is you do when we're not around."

I grind my teeth. Clench my jaw. To keep from calling her the crusty crotch crack she's acting like. Too much? My bad. Blame the good Dr. Seuss—we've been reading him a lot in my house.

I take a deep breath. Then I close my eyes and tilt my head

back. I'll wait Dolores out. She'll have to leave at some point. Or I can use the cum-stained complimentary pillow to smother her.

The thought makes me smile.

Dee-Dee and Kate talk. And talk. After a few minutes, the sounds blend together in my male ears like those of Charlie Brown's faceless teacher. " . . . wa wa wah wah wanh . . . Matthew's birthday present . . . wa wa wanh . . . wasn't sure . . . wah wah wa wa . . . came through last minute . . . wa wa wah wanh . . . see his face . . . wa wa wah . . . so surprised . . . wa wanh . . ."

Gifts are important to women. But what I've come to realize is—at least for some of them—it's not the actual gift that matters. Or even how much cash you shelled out for it. It's all about the effort. Symbolism. How much thought you put into getting it for them.

For instance, if I were to hunt down a napkin from the bar where Kate and I first met? Then, if I had it matted and framed and gave it to her as an anniversary present? I'm pretty sure she'd fuck me into a coma to show her gratitude.

It's still just a napkin. But to Kate—it means so much more.

Last year for my birthday, she got my initials waxed into her bush. I was touched. Talk about a great gift—creative and practical. Anyway, with mild curiosity I open my eyes and ask Delores, "What are you giving him?"

She grins smugly. "Only the greatest gift a woman can give the man she loves."

I take my best guess. "Anal?"

Kate covers her eyes.

Dee-Dee's smile turns into a scowl. "No—pig. I'm giving him the gift of health. My acupuncturist cleared her schedule. She's going to work on Matthew the whole day."

I laugh. Because this explains so much.

"*That's* your gift? Really? It's the guy's birthday and you're gonna make him get needles stuck in his face all day? What are you gonna get him for Christmas—a colonoscopy?"

Kate clarifies, "Drew, the acupuncture is to get Matthew to stop smoking."

Yep, Matthew's a smoker. Statistically, if you don't start by the age of eighteen, you never will. But my buddy's the exception to this rule. His habit began in college—during a particularly stressful game of *Madden NFL* football.

Matthew's kept it in the closet, however. His parents don't know. Because Frank sucks back two packs a day—and like any smoker, he'd break every one of his kid's fingers if he found out he was doing it too.

I put my hands up in surrender. "I take it back, Dee—it's a stupendous gift. Anything to help Matthew kick the cancer sticks is a good thing."

She practically pats herself on the back. "Thank you, Drew."

"You're welcome. Now that we've gotten that settled, could you please—and I mean this in the nicest way possible—go the fuck away?"

She's not smiling anymore. "No. I told you—this is *my* time. *My* Kate time."

Fast Times at Ridgemont High appears in my head. "Whatever, Mr. Hand."

Kate reaches over and touches my leg. "Drew, maybe you should just go hang out with the guys for the rest of the flight."

I stamp my foot. And point at Dee-Dee. "How come *she* gets Kate time? Where's *my* Kate time? I want Kate time too!"

Dee-Dee answers, "You'll be getting a whole bunch of Kate time next week. It's called a honeymoon, dumbass."

I glare at her. "You suck."

She rubs a finger over her lips lasciviously. "That I do. Frequently. Matthew doesn't complain."

I grimace. "Now I'm nauseous. Kate, will you rub my stomach?"

Kate smiles. Her voice takes on that motherly, condescending tone she gets when she's asking James to behave. "Yes, Drew—I'll rub your stomach, and any other body part you want me to . . . when we get to the hotel."

I sigh and resign myself to not getting laid. Just as I start to sink into a deep depression, Jack's voice echoes throughout the cabin.

"Dude! Check it out! I've got porn on my in-flight entertainment system!"

Someone yelling "porn" in an enclosed space is akin to an alarm's going off in a firehouse at midnight. Four pairs of feet scramble in Jack's direction, including mine. Maybe guy time won't be so bad, after all.

I know what you're thinking. *Stop wasting my time. Can we skip the bullshit and get to the good stuff already?*

I'm working on it.

Besides, I think you should enjoy the good times while they last. I did. I have a feeling things are going to get real crazy—real quick—from here on out. 'Cause our next stop? That's Vegas, baby. And there's a reason it's called Sin City.

Chapter 6

When it comes to swanky hotel rooms, you might think the penthouse is top-of-the-line. In most cases, you'd be right. But the Bellagio has something better. The villa. It's the kind of place only royalty, heads of state, and highly overrated actors get to stay. Five bedrooms, formal dining room, office, library, and a huge kitchen—all trimmed in elegant woods and marbles—decked out with the finest appliances, accessories, and Italian fabrics. It even comes with a full-service maid and butler staff.

Money can't buy happiness—but it makes it a hell of a lot easier to stay happy.

Since we're the guests of honor, Kate and I get the master suite. Our adjoining bathroom has a steam shower and huge Jacuzzi that I definitely plan on putting to good use later. Steven and Alexandra, Delores and Matthew, each pair gets a room too—complete with fireplace and king-size bed. Erin claims a slightly smaller room with a queen, while Jack and Warren bunk together in the last room.

It's a good thing their room has two double beds, because if there's one thing a guy will never do, it's share a bed with another dude. Sleeping naked on sharp gravel? Totally acceptable, when faced with the risk of waking up to a loaded rifle in your back.

After the butler—we'll call him Mr. Belvedere—gives us the grand tour and the maids take our luggage to unpack, the nine of us relax in the living room, talking about the agenda for the day.

Sitting on the dark brown love seat, with Delores on his lap, Matthew goes first. "There's a water-volleyball tournament down at the pool in twenty minutes. I figured we'd start there—get our burn on. And they're having a pig-roast barbecue—you know how I love a good swine."

All the guys nod their consent.

Dee-Dee begins, "Our goddess party starts at five. . . ."

Goddess parties . . . for guys they're a dream—mythical. Like the fabled pot of gold at the end of the rainbow, or the topless pillow fight at a sleepover. It's pretty much a female-only sex party, minus the actual sex. Legend has it there's a wide array of toys for sale—dildos, vibrators, bondage gear, and lingerie. And there are lessons—women are instructed on all kinds of acquired skills, such as deep throat, masturbation, pole dancing.

". . . but before that, we ladies have appointments at the spa, to get beautified for tonight."

I run my hand through Kate's dark hair as she sits beside me on the couch. "That's a waste of time," I tell her. "You can't improve perfection."

She blushes slightly. Still *so* fucking adorable.

Dee-Dee counters, "You say that now—but wait until you see us after. We're gonna get wrapped, waxed, plucked, and massaged. I swear, Kate—after Ricardo works you over? You'll never be the same. It's like being touched by an orgasm."

My curiosity gets the best of me. "Who's Ricardo?"

"Kate's massage therapist."

Huh. "Ricardo's a weird name for a woman."

Delores rolls her eyes. "Well, yeah, it would be—but Ricardo's all man. He's got the body of a Greek god, like Arnold Schwarzenegger in his steroid days. And he knows how to use it—especially his hands."

Some guys would be okay with this situation. Men who are laid-back like Matthew or understanding like Steven. They'd kiss their lady on the cheek and say, "*Have a good time, honey.*" But—despite my emotional growth these last years—that's just not how I roll.

So what I say is "Yeah, that's not fucking happening."

Kate puts her hand on my leg. "Drew, it's just a massage."

"I'm aware of that. Two words—*happy ending*. Two more words—*no way*."

Alexandra tries to be helpful. "Relax, little brother. There's no reason to be jealous."

I open my arms wide. "Who's jealous? I'm not jealous—'cause it's not fucking happening." I turn to Kate and explain calmly, "You really think I'm gonna be able to just sit here knowing you're out there—with your goodies covered only by a thin cotton towel—while Ricardo-frigging-Montalbán has his hands all over you? Making you moan? Screw that. All your moans belong to me—they're paid in full with that rock on your finger."

Dee-Dee holds her hand out to Matthew. "I knew he wouldn't be able to handle it. Pay up."

He pulls his wallet out and slaps a twenty in her palm. I shake my head in disappointment at him. "You thought I'd be okay with this?"

He shrugs.

My eyes narrow. "I don't even know you anymore."

"Ricardo's awesome, man. His hands are magic. If I was gay, I would totally enter into a civil union with him."

From the recliner, Steven joins the discussion. "You let a dude give you a rubdown? Have you considered the possibility that you're already gay?"

"Blow me."

Steven laughs. "See, that's what I mean. These subliminal messages are tickling my gaydar." He holds his finger out, pointing to each guy in the room. "Beep. Beep. Beep . . ." Then he points at Matthew. "Beeeeeeeeeeeeeeeeeeeeeeeep."

Billy and Jack crack up, and Steven gives them a high five. Matthew makes the jerk-off sign with his hand. Which doesn't help his case much.

Kate brings us back on topic. "This is really a problem for you?"

I nod. "Absolutely. It'll taint my memory of the entire weekend."

She sighs. And turns toward Delores. "Switch my appointment."

Dee-Dee looks appalled. "You're not serious?" She throws her hands up in the air. "And so it begins. You're not even married yet, and he's already controlling you—dictating what you can and can't do."

I jump to Kate's defense. "She's respecting my goddamn feelings. That's how a mature, healthy relationship works. You should try it sometime."

"I'm extremely considerate of Matthew's feelings!"

Kate jumps in. "Dee, we're here to have fun, not torture my fiancé."

Dee-Dee pouts. "But torturing him *is* my idea of fun. Party pooper." Still, she grabs the phone and calls the spa.

Kate nestles into my side, resting her head on my shoulder. I pull her closer and kiss the top her head. "Thank you."

"You're welcome."

I grin. "When you get back from your primping, I want some of that Kate time you owe me."

She lifts her head and whispers, "Does this, by chance, involve finishing what we started on the plane?"

I nod slowly. "It does—and I guarantee it will be a spectacular finish."

"It always is." She leans forward, kissing me playfully, her tongue grazing and teasing.

When she pulls back, I lick my bottom lip, savoring the taste of her. "Bet your ass it is."

Warren interrupts our flirtatious moment. "So, before we split up, does anybody wanna like . . . get high?"

I'm not a big fan of drugs, even the recreational kind. With alcohol, you can pace yourself—have a drink or two, then slow down and enjoy the buzz. Or you can go full throttle and down five quick shots. In either case, there's control over how shitfaced you want to be.

But drugs are like a train without a conductor. Once you're on, you're going for a ride—no slowing down, no getting off if you change your mind. Dee-Dee doesn't share my sentiments. No surprise there.

She sits next to her cousin on arm of the couch. "Thank God—I thought you'd never ask."

Warren reaches into his pocket and pulls out a clear baggie that contains a few prerolled joints, some loose marijuana, and a small, brightly colored bowl pipe.

Erin asks, "Where'd you get that from?"

"I brought it from New York." His brow furrows as he clarifies, "Well, technically, I brought it from California to New York, and then here. It's good shit—high-level medical grade. The janitor at my music studio has glaucoma."

"But how did you get it past airport security?" my sister questions.

Warren explains proudly, "I keep it in my boxer briefs. That way, if I get picked for one of those scanner things, it just looks like the downstairs dreadlocks need a trim."

I raise my eyebrows. "Now *there's* a backup plan. If the music career tanks, you can always become a drug mule." Drug smugglers have an extremely high rate of early, violent death. *Awesome.*

Warren passes Dee-Dee a joint and she lights up. Matthew makes his way over. "I could go for a hit of herb."

Erin is hesitant. "I've never smoked marijuana before."

Warren tries to be reassuring. "Then you've come to the right place. We're all friends in the dope show."

She still looks nervous, so I tell her, "Just say no, Erin. Only losers get high." I point my thumb at Warren. "You really want to end up like Exhibit A over there?"

Delores holds her hands up like claws. "Peer pressure! Come on, Erin—you have to try it at least once. Live a little, girlfriend."

"And that would be Exhibit B."

Erin takes a big breath and looks at me with wide, approval-seeking eyes. "I think I'm gonna try it. I mean . . . sometimes you just have to say, 'What the fuck?' . . . right, Drew?"

You can't argue with a *Risky Business* quote. I shrug my shoulders in surrender, and Erin joins the rest of the stoners.

Jack's not interested. "No thanks, man. I'm all about keeping the toxins out of my system these days."

Alexandra declines as well, with a wave of her hand. Steven, however, says, "Sure, why not? I'll relive my misspent youth."

Alexandra snaps, "What do you mean *relive*? You're a man—you're still living your misspent youth."

My brother-in-law holds out his hand to Warren. "Make mine a double."

Warren passes Steven a full bowl and a lighter, while Matthew offers Kate the joint. She shakes her head. "Maybe later."

I walk across the room, open a window, and turn on the ceiling fan.

Warren asks, "What about you, Evans? You down?"

I snort. "Like I'd ever put something in my mouth that hitched a ride next to your sweaty balls. I'd rather kiss a jungle elephant's ass."

Warren takes a long drag, and puffs of smoke escape his lips as he mocks me. "Narc."

I deadpan, "Yeah, that's me. On my off days I hang out with Johnny Depp down at 21 Jump Street."

Already feeling the effects of the high, Matthew giggles. And announces to the whole room, "Nah, Andrew's cool. But him and Mary Jane don't get along. He tried her once in college. It didn't work out."

Kate leans forward. "I've never heard that story."

"It wasn't exactly one of my finer moments."

Matthew laughs louder. "He took four hits, then started running around the house locking all the doors and windows. He thought his old man was gonna show up, or the SWAT team was gonna drop out of the sky. Then he had a panic attack."

"I did not have a frigging panic attack."

Matthew's eyes meet mine. "Dude, I thought I was gonna

have to haul your ass to the emergency room. You looked like you were going into cardiac fucking arrest."

Everyone has a good chuckle at my expense—even Kate.

Warren nods his head happily. "Evans can't handle the weed. Good to know. Now, if I ever want to mess with you, I know just how to do it."

Friends are supposed to rag on each other. It's one of the benefits of knowing everything about a person—all their accomplishments, all their embarrassing, dirty little secrets.

But that's a hammer that swings both ways.

"Keep on walking down memory lane, Matthew. There's a few potholes I could dig up on you too."

He spreads his arms wide. "I'm an open book."

I smile devilishly. "You sure about that?"

"Bring it, chump."

I turn toward his wife. "Hey, Dee, Matthew ever tell you about the time he was so trashed, he pissed in Kelly Macallister's mouth while she was giving him a blow job?"

Matthew sobers immediately.

Steven doubles over laughing.

"Ewwww," Erin squeals. "That's so gross."

"That's how he got his nickname in our fraternity—Golden Shower Fisher."

Alexandra looks both sickened and amused.

Jack snorts, "Nasty."

Kate grimaces and covers her ears.

Delores laughs at first, then turns to her husband and confesses, "I'm ruined. I'll never be able to suck you off again without thinking of that story."

Matthew glares at me good-naturedly, "You're a dickwad, man."

I just grin. "That's what friends are for, buddy."

Ten minutes later, Erin lies feet up in the recliner with heavy-lidded eyes. She raises one arm slowly, then the other. "This is great. I'm so relaxed."

Steven's face is slack as he motions toward the shiny grand piano in the corner. "Hey, Billy, why don't you play something?"

Yes, asswipe can also play the piano. Just keep in mind—he may be a multifaceted tool, but he's still a fucking tool.

Dee pipes up, "Good idea. Nothing goes better with a quality high than some smooth tunes. Make it mellow, cuz."

Shit-for-brains gets up, settles himself on the piano bench, cracks his knuckles, and starts to play. After a few bars of instrumental, he starts to sing "Someone Like You" by Adele. It figures he'd choose a chick song.

As he croons the last line before the chorus—the one about things not being over between him and his former love, my good mood sours like milk left out of the fridge too long. This is why I always have, do now, and will forever hate Warren's guts. Because, despite Matthew's story about my experience with marijuana, I'm not a paranoid guy. I'm observant. Intelligent. Goddamn smart enough to know why—out of all the motherfucking songs he could have played—he picked this one.

And more important—I know whom he's playing it for.

There are no accidents. Body language and Freudian slips have meaning. They're our subconscious's way of showing how we really feel. What we really want. And somewhere, deep down in Warren's puny brain and inadequate heart—I think he still wants Kate.

Look at her face now. It's the same look she always gets when she watches him sing. Her head's tilted slightly, a small smile sits on her lips, and her eyes swim with a mixture of pride and wonderment. Admiration. And possibly, remembered affection. Even though I know she doesn't have those feelings for him anymore, even though I know she chose me—she loves me more—it pisses me off. Badly.

Because the only person I've ever looked at like that—in my entire life—is her.

As he plays the final note, I swallow my resentment down. Matthew, Steven, Erin, Dee-Dee, and Kate clap. Alexandra actually wipes a tear from her eye.

Jack says, "Damn you're good. That music shit must make you a righteous pussy hound. Tonight, Billy, you're my wingman."

Warren nods shyly. "Sure, man."

Then I stand up. "Now that I've gotten my dose of estrogen for the day, how about we head to the pool and check out that barbecue? I don't know about you guys, but I'm more than ready for the first of many rounds."

Everyone agrees.

I keep Kate close to me as we all head to our respective rooms for a quick clothing change. And prepare to go our separate ways.

Chapter 7

The barbecue at the adults-only pool is in full swing. There's music, sunshine, bikinis as far as the eye can see—and some I wish I didn't have to. Remember, ladies, two-piece bathing suits are a privilege, not a right.

We rent an enclosed cabana near the bar and settle down at the circular, umbrella-covered table in front of it. Our round of beers arrives and we hang out waiting for our turn in the volleyball tournament. For men, team sports have the power to inspire a warlike, us-against-them mentality. It's like spending the night in a foxhole—an instant bonding experience. Even if you don't like each other—hell, even if you can't stand each other—you close ranks, pick up the slack where you have to. Because you're in the same platoon, and anyone who's not with you is against you. They're the enemy.

Why am I telling you this? You'll understand shortly.

For now, I take a sip of my beer and focus on my sullen-faced brother-in-law. I get right to the point: "What's going on with you and my sister?"

He's not surprised by the question. But he's reluctant. "I don't want to talk about it."

"*You don't want to talk about it?* What? Did you grow a vagina on the walk over? I suppose next you'll tell me you're *fine*? Don't be a bitch, Steven—talk. What's up?"

He rubs his hand down his face and stares at the pool for a minute. Deliberating. Then he turns toward us and leans forward, elbows on the table. "All right. It started about two weeks ago. For a couple days, Alexandra had been in a rotten mood. But I wasn't worried—she just gets like that sometimes. And then I found something in the bathroom trash can . . . a pregnancy test."

Sympathetic groans roll across the table like the wave at a football game. "She's never gonna let you out of the house again."

"You gotta space the kids out, Steven. If you have them too close together, one is bound to fall through the cracks."

"Now it's gonna be three against two—you're screwed."

Steven holds up his hand. "It was negative. Alexandra's not pregnant." He takes a swig from his beer. "But when I asked her about it, she went ballistic. Yelling at me about how I don't understand her—how I shouldn't worry about kids because I can have them until I'm seventy. And how men pretty much suck in general. Ever since then, she's been unbearable. It's like she's just looking for any excuse to be pissed off at me."

Matthew advises, "Maybe she needs a break. You know—a night out to feel more like a woman and less like a mom?"

Steven shakes his head. "Already thought of that. I set up an overnight in the Hamptons—had my dad lined up to take the kids and everything. She shot me down—wanted no part of it.

Then she bitched me out for making plans without consulting her."

Jack snorts, "Can't say I'm surprised. No offense, dude, but Alexandra's always been a cold fish."

I don't take exception to his comment because I can see why he'd think like that.

Steven's voice takes on a soft, sad tone. Wistful. "But she's not, though. That's just a front she puts up. The real Alexandra is warm . . . and funny . . . and she'd go to ends of the earth for the people she loves. Up until two weeks ago, that included me. But lately . . . it doesn't. And I don't know why."

I pinch the bridge of my nose and sigh. "You gotta fix this, Steven. You can't do this to me—not now."

He doesn't take it well. "You? What the hell does this have to do with *you*, Drew?"

I point my finger at him accusingly. "You and Alexandra are my gold standard. You're the only reason I'm not shitting my pants about marrying Kate next week. Because you're my proof that marriage can actually work."

Steven's brow wrinkles. "Your parents have been married for forty years."

I wave my hand. "They don't count. They're old—no one else will have them."

Matthew asks, "What about me and Dee?"

"I give you another year—tops."

Matthew just shrugs. Because he doesn't give a damn what other people think—even me.

Now, Alexandra may be my sister—but Steven is more than a brother-in-law. He's a friend—one of my best. Which makes placing loyalties a sticky situation. So if I have to take sides? I'm going with Mackenzie and Thomas. "And there's no frigging way

I'm letting my niece and nephew grow up in a broken home. You gotta talk to her, Steven—work it out."

He pushes his chair back—frustrated. "I've tried! Don't you think I've tried? I've kissed her ass for the last two weeks. . . ."

I close my eyes and hold up my hand. "Please—easy on the mental pictures."

"I've tried everything I can think of . . . but I'm not gonna try anymore. If she wants to work it out, when she wants to talk—she's gonna have to come to me. I'm putting my foot down. I have some pride, you know."

Looks as if I'll be taking matters into my own hands. "I'll have a sit-down with my sister when we get back—find out what the hell her deal is."

Steven is vehement. "No, Drew. This is between me and my wife. Stay out of it."

I back off. "All right. Relax—don't have a coronary." But I still plan on talking to Alexandra. If you want something done right, you have to fucking do it yourself.

We're all silent for a minute.

Steven says, "Look—I don't want this to bring us all down. Just shelve it. For tonight, let's just have a good time—like the old days. The only thing I want to think about is getting hammered and having fun. GTG all the way."

Matthew laughs. Because, like me, he hasn't heard those letters in years. And they bring back some pretty awesome memories.

He fist-taps Steven. "Fuckin' A right—GTG."

Warren asks, "What's GTG?"

I smile. "It was our monogram back in the day."

"What's it stand for?"

I wiggle my eyebrows. "Good-time guys."

Later, going into the fourth round of the water-volleyball tournament, we're in first place. Kicking ass and taking names. With only three more matches until the championships. It's fun. Physical. We exert ourselves but have enough time in between games to kick back, socialize, and down a few drinks.

Steven is currently getting down on the makeshift dance floor to "Blurred Lines." Can you see him over there? Pointing his fingers John Travolta style and thrusting his hips in time to the beat? It's not smooth or cool, but somehow Steven still comes off looking like the fucking man. The hip-shaking, hand-clapping, giggling girls surrounding him are loving it.

Across the opposite end of the pool is a loud, big-drinking divorce celebration, to which Jack invited himself, and he ended up getting some action in the hot tub from the divorcée herself.

Now he's back at the table with Matthew and me. We've been playing it mellow. Despite a few panty-dropping offers, we've made it clear our interests lie in hanging out—not hooking up. Surprisingly, Warren has turned out to be the heavy hitter in the poontang department.

Well . . . kind of. After our second win, he disappeared with a chick into the cabana. They came out half an hour later, retying their bathing suits. Fifteen minutes ago, he dove back in again—with girl number two.

I'm not impressed because . . . how can I put this without making you want to snip my balls off with a pair of garden shears? . . . girl number one was . . . of the rotund persuasion. A jolly girl. The kind who has to broadcast an entertaining personality because she's severely lacking in the shape department. Don't get me wrong, big girls have their place in society too. *Fat bottomed girls, you make the rockin' world go round,* and all that.

And every guy has a type. One man's hog is another man's hottie. I've always preferred my women on the petite side—they're easier to flip around and maneuver into just the right position. But I don't think Warren has a passion for the plumpies. I mean, he held on to Kate for a decade, and she never went through a chubby phase—I've seen pictures.

Plus, Warren's girl number two was totally at the other end of the spectrum. Superskinny, with a rack as flat as a surfboard, and a hook nose that suggested a strong relation to the bald eagle.

Pencil-dick himself emerges from the cabana with a satisfied grin. He sits down at the table and takes a long drag from his beer. Matthew, Jack, and I just stare at him.

He looks back and forth between us. "What?"

I jerk my chin toward girl number two as she walks back to her table of equally unattractive friends. Subpars tend to stick together.

"What's with you and the scary sisters?"

"What do you mean?"

"I mean your first hookup made Snooki look like Miss America. And that last chick is probably next of kin to the Wicked Witch of the West."

He sneers defensively. "She wasn't that bad."

Matthew and Jack cough. "Butter face . . . butter face."

Warren asks, "What's a butter face?"

I roll my eyes at his ignorance. "It means everything is hot—but. Her. Face. Get it? And I think that's pretty generous, considering there's nothing boner-worthy about a woman with the hips of a ten-year-old boy."

Jack suggests, "Maybe it's a fetish. You like to bump uglies with the uglies, Billy?"

"No. I don't have a thing for ugly girls."

I beg to differ. Still, I give him the chance to explain himself. "Then why are they the only ones you're hitting on?"

Warren squirms uncomfortably. "They're just . . . easier. I like a sure thing."

Matthew says, "You sold out Giants fucking Stadium six months ago. For you they should *all* be sure things."

Warren avoids eye contact and picks at the label on his beer. "I don't know. It's like . . . I was with Kate for a long time . . ."

As if I could fucking forget.

". . . and I never really had a chance to practice my skills, you know? And chicks in LA? They're bitches, man—they're hot and they know it. So, it's less intimidating if I stick with the easy scores."

There's a story in the Bible about a guy who was a real mean bastard. One day he was walking down the road, and God knocked him on his ass. This blinding light came from the sky, and a booming voice shouted down from the heavens, telling him what he needed to do. How to fix his life.

That's what this moment is like for me. An epiphany. A divine revelation.

If I can find Warren a girl of his own . . . if I can teach him the secrets of scoring quality pieces of ass . . . maybe he'll be so distracted, he'll finally stop sniffing around Kate. And maybe—just maybe—I'll be rid of him. For good.

I have seen the path to the promised land, boys and girls. And it's lined with pussy.

Energized by the prospect of a Warren-less existence, I propose, "I can help you with that, you know."

"With getting girls?"

I nod. "Getting top-notch girls. The kind of females you've only seen in magazines and wet dreams. I can teach you how to make it happen. Once you taste gourmet, you'll never munch junk food again."

Jack tells Warren, "Jump all over this, man. You'd be learning from the best. Evans is the master—before he gets married, they should bronze his dick, like DiMaggio's cleats."

Jack's praise is flattering. And a little disturbing.

Still, Warren looks suspicious. "Why would you want to help me?"

I shrug. "I'm a sucker for a lost cause—St. Jude always was my favorite saint. Plus, you're Kate's little buddy. If I help you out, I score points with her. And that's always a good thing."

He seems satisfied with my answer, so I start with the basics. "What's your game?"

"My what?"

"Your game plan. How do you approach these *gorgeous* LA women? What do you say?"

He scratches his head, like the dumbfuck monkey he is. "Well, sometimes I'll rush over, looking surprised, and I'll say, '*Are you all right? Did you hurt yourself? That fall from heaven was far.*' "

The guys and I start laughing straightaway. But Warren doesn't. Then we stop.

I ask, "I'm sorry—were you serious?"

He looks away, slightly pissed. "Forget this."

I implore him, "No, we won't laugh anymore. I want to help. What else?"

He debates answering for a second. "Sometimes I tell a joke."

Matthew looks perplexed. "A joke?"

"Yeah—you know—'This guy walks into a bar . . .' Shit like that."

I nod slowly. "Right. I can see why you think that would work . . . because every woman wants to screw Bozo the Clown."

Then we start laughing again.

Warren growls, "Fuck you guys. I'm out of here." He starts to get up.

"Wait—don't go. Come on, man, we're just busting your balls."

Reluctantly Warren sits back down.

I begin my tutorial. "First mistake—you're trying too hard. Women can smell desperation like a dog smells fear. And to them, it reeks like shit. You have to be calm. Confident. Like . . . when we were kids, Matthew's uncle used to take us camping. At the campground there was a lake with all these sunnies swimming around, that all the kids would try to catch. There was this one annoying little prick who wanted to catch the most fish—so he brought a net. He'd slam it into the water over and over, but he never caught any fish. He just scared them away. I, on the other hand, would bring a little bag of bread crumbs. I'd drop in just a few at a time—a small taste. Then I'd sit back and wait. After a minute or two, all the fish would come to me. You see what I'm saying?"

Monkey-boy nods. "Yeah . . ." Then he stops. "No, actually. Not really."

This is going to be harder than I thought. And the really scary thing? If Kate and I die together in a fiery collision? This dumbass is third in line to raise my kid.

Forget global warming—*that's* the thought that keeps me up at night.

"You're thinking too much." I take a drink of my beer. "Forget the lines. Forget the goddamn jokes. Women aren't that complicated. You just have to figure out what they want to hear. Then, tell it to them. You do that, and even the hottest knees will part like the Red Sea."

He digests my words for a moment. "So I should tell a chick I'll listen to her demo tape? Maybe get her a recording contract?"

I shake my head. "No. Rule number one—don't make promises you can't or have no intention of keeping. Play it straight—anything else is just a scumbag move. And it's the easiest way to turn a semi-normal chick into a stalker. After the deal gets sealed, if you're in a jam and need an exit strategy, ask for her phone number—but don't actually say you're going to call. It'll be assumed, but that's not your problem." I take another drink of beer. "It's all about the moment—screw tomorrow. Decipher what she wants, right then and there. Some chicks actually want a dickhead—they get off on being treated like crap."

Don't even think about telling me I'm wrong. Where do you think the whole "nice guys finish last" thing came from? Because deep down, some women live for drama.

"Some just want a shoulder to cry on, or a good time. Listen to what they say, watch how they say it, and show them that, at least for the night, you're exactly what they're looking for."

Matthew says, "He looks confused, Drew. Maybe a little demonstration is in order?"

"Good idea."

I scan the pool area and spot a waitress scurrying across the concrete. She's got dark, curly hair, pale skin with a hint of freckles. She fills out her uniform nicely—a white blouse tied in a knot at the waist, high and tight, black shorts that look as if they were stolen from Hooters, and black heels. *Bingo.*

I point her out. "What do you think of her?"

Jack comments, "I'd bang her."

Warren agrees, "Yeah. She's cute."

I wave my hand and call the waitress over. With pad and pen ready she asks, "Hey, guys, what can I do for you?"

I'll never understand why women set themselves up like that. Try to think like a man, for God's sake. When a red-blooded guy hears this question? He immediately thinks of at least eight different things you could "do" for him, in about ten different positions.

I give her my most charming smile. "Could you bring us a bottle of Jäger, honey? And five shot glasses please. Take your time, you look busy. We're not in a rush."

"No problem. Coming right up."

She turns away and walks to the bar.

Jack stares. "I hate it when they leave, but I love to watch them go."

Warren's staring at her ass too.

So I smack him. *Slap.* To get his attention . . . and . . . because it's fun.

"Focus. Look at her."

"I *was* looking at her!"

"Not just at her ass—look at the whole package."

He glares at me, touching his cheek. Then he watches the waitress.

"See how she's rubbing her lower back? And wiping the sweat from her forehead? How she shifts her weight from one foot to the other? What do you think she needs right now?"

His face scrunches up with concentration.

After a minute, I can't resist. "Don't hurt yourself."

He sighs. "I don't know—she looks like she could use a nap."

I smile. "There's hope for you yet. A nap would be good, but you can't give that to her. What you can do is make her feel important. Valued. Show her that you appreciate her as a woman, not just a server. Chicks eat that shit up."

Waitress girl starts to head back over, balancing a bottle and shot glasses on a tray one-handedly. Before she reaches us, I hiss a warning at Warren—just to be safe. "And don't even *think* about telling tales to Kate that I'm screwing around. This is for purely educational purposes only. It means nothing to me."

That's the absolute truth. It's like . . . acting. I would have made a great actor. The Broadway kind. Because no matter what an actor feels for his leading lady in real life—when that curtain rises, he performs. Convincingly.

She arrives at our table. "Here we go, guys."

As she sets out the glasses, I ask, "Is it always this crazy around here?"

"Not always. There's a podiatrist convention in town this weekend, so we're swamped." She brushes a hair from her face. "The tips are good though, so I can't complain."

"Sure you can. Everyone deserves to bitch once in a while. I'm all ears."

She smiles and pours our drinks.

"Better yet—how about you sit down for a few minutes? Take a load off. Have a drink with us? You look like you could use one."

She's tempted. But then she glances over her shoulder at the balding, heavyset guy behind the bar. "It's sweet of you to ask—but I can't. My boss wouldn't like it."

"Sweet is my middle name." I jerk my thumb toward the bar, "He your boss?"

She frowns. "That's him. Harry's a total slave driver."

I stand and hold up a finger. "Don't go anywhere."

I jog over to Harry. "Hey, man, my friends and I are looking to have a quick drink with our waitress."

He looks over at our table. "With Felicia?"

"Yeah, Felicia"—or, whatever—"and we're willing to pay for her time. What's a ten-minute break gonna cost me?"

"Fifty bucks."

"Done." I slap the money on the bar and beat it back to the table quickly—before the price goes up. Then I put my sexy face back on.

I pull out a chair and motion for the waitress to sit. "You're all set."

She looks surprised. "No kidding?" She looks at Harry, who gives her a nod, then she sits down gratefully. "Wow, you convinced Harry to give me a break? You must be very good."

I chuckle wickedly. "Baby, you have no idea."

I sit in my chair and raise my shot glass. Everyone follows suit and we down them together. Then I pour another for the waitress. We chat casually for a few minutes. She tells me about her dreams of becoming a showgirl, which were put on hold because of her mother's emphysema. I listen oh so attentively and nod at all the right times.

Then I dig a little deeper. "That's a lot for a lady to have on her shoulders. Does your husband help out?"

She drinks her second shot and shakes her head. "No husband."

"A boyfriend, then?"

"Not one of them, either. Who has the time?"

Then I go in for the kill. "A great girl like you doesn't have a boyfriend? That's a damn shame. Still, you should make time to blow off a little steam. Let loose. Have a good time with a good guy."

She licks the alcohol off her lips. "I squeeze in a good time here and there. When it's worth it."

See her suggestive smirk? The invitation in her big, hazel eyes? That's her signal—telling me she thinks *I'm* worth it. That if I offer to help her blow off some steam in any fashion I can think of, she's up for it.

That also concludes our presentation for the day.

I glance at my watch. "Ten minutes are up. I wouldn't want you to get into trouble with your boss."

She blinks. "Oh—right."

Then she stands up—but doesn't leave right away. "I'm done here in a few hours. Are you guys going to stick around?" She asks all of us, but she's looking at me.

I let her down easy. Because that's the kind of gentleman I am. "Unfortunately, no. We'll be heading out soon and we're busy all night. But it was a pleasure talking to you."

Back in the day, I would have kissed her hand for good measure. But these days my lips are for Kate alone.

Her shoulders sag. "Okay . . . well . . . thanks for the drink."

"Anytime, honey. Don't work too hard."

She walks away, sneaking a peek back over at our table as she goes.

I turn my attention to Warren and spread my arms wide. "And *that* is how it's done."

I toss back a shot. My voice is strained after it burns down my throat. "If I was interested, I'd hang around awhile. And if no other opportunities presented themselves, I'd take her home, bang her for a few hours, and leave her smiling."

Warren suggests, with a hint of awe, "Yeah. Or you could bring her up to your room for a quickie."

Jack, Matthew, and I simultaneously exclaim, "Nooooo."

I correct him, "With the high-end women you're going to be scoring? You're gonna want to take your time. And—rule number two—always have an escape route. Never take a girl back to your home turf. It could take a forklift to get her the fuck out."

Jack shudders. "One time I had to call the cops. And when they dragged her out, the broad was still clinging to my bedsheets. That's a mistake you only make once."

Warren nods. "You make it seem so easy."

"Getting laid is supposed to be easy," I tell him. "None of us would be here if it wasn't. God gave men instincts—even you. Just relax and let them lead you."

I slap him on the back. Harder than I have to. "Now, young Skywalker, your training is complete. Tonight—you become a Jedi."

He grins. "Cool. Thanks, man." Then he cocks his thumb toward the restroom. "I gotta hit the john."

Jack stands. "And I see a new lucky lady. I'll be back."

After they leave, Matthew's eyes burn a hole in my face.

I return his stare. "What?"

"A few hours ago you could barely stand to be in the same room with the guy, and now you're giving him pussy pointers. Why are you really helping him, Drew?"

"I'm a helpful guy."

He continues to stare, waiting for me to elaborate.

"And . . . if Warren's occupied with his own snatch . . . he'll stay away from Kate."

Matthew's head rolls back with a groan. "Dude—you're still hung up on that? Let it go, man."

"Did you not hear the same song I did?"

His voice rises with exasperation. "So fucking what? It was a song. Kate is marrying *you*—you have a *son* together." He cups his hands around his mouth like a megaphone. "Get over it."

I rub the back of my neck. "I am. I am over it. But . . . when I see him . . . when I see *them* together—it drives me nuts."

"Why?"

"Because I still think he has feelings for Kate."

"Again—why?"

I grind my teeth. And clench my hands. When I open my mouth, the God's honest truth comes tumbling out. "Because I would never let her go, Matthew. Ever. No matter what happened—no matter what I did, I'd keep hoping, trying, until she came back to me."

Matthew nods compassionately. "And *that* is why *you* are marrying Kate, and Warren is not. Because he *was* able to let her go. It wasn't the forever kind of relationship, it was the for-right-now kind. And he did get over her. It's the same way for Kate. So stop torturing yourself—and the rest of us—and just fucking enjoy it. You won. She's yours."

I think about his words for a moment. And then I shrug. "Either way, no harm, no foul. I get peace of mind, Warren gets his pickup skills upgraded, and Kate will be pleasantly surprised that I'm not jumping at the chance to put him in a shallow grave. Everybody wins, right?"

Matthew nods thoughtfully and finishes his drink.

Over the speaker system, the lifeguard calls our team number, and we get ready to nail the game.

Chapter 8

By the time we head back to the villa—as the returning water-volleyball champions we are—afternoon has slipped into dusk. It's my favorite time of day. The sun is setting and the air smells like summer—a mix of earth and chlorine and freshly cut grass. I swipe my card through the security gate surrounding the house and walk toward the front door.

Something in the window catches Jack's eye, and he freezes. "What the hell . . ."

I follow his gaze through the window. I see the girls in the library, sitting in a circular formation on chairs dragged in from the dining room. They're wearing long, pink, satiny robes and open-back, fuzzy, black heels. In the center of the circle stands a tall, fiftyish blonde in full black-leather dominatrix attire. She's sort of hot—in an aging-hooker, been-around-the-block, her-pussy-is-probably-as-wide-as-the-Lincoln-Tunnel kind of way.

I whisper excitedly, "Goddess party."

See? Dreams really do come true.

Matthew fist-pumps. "Yes!"

Like SEAL Team Six, we stealthily invade the villa single-file. Once inside, we line up—totem-pole style—in front of the library's mahogany double doors. Without making a sound, I crack the door—just a little. Just enough to watch and listen. In one hand, dominatrix lady holds a mini, purple vibrator—in the other, a matching remote control.

"We call this the Master. You insert the vibrator into your panties, and your gentleman takes possession of the controller. It's noiseless and discreet, but powerful. With the remote, he can alternate speed and pressure at his discretion. . . ."

Matthew whispers, "I have *got* to get me one of those."

I murmur, "I'm gonna get five." I envision our weekly staff meetings in the conference room taking on a whole new meaning.

Dominatrix lady goes on, "And now, ladies, let's continue our oral instruction. Your bananas, please."

Instantly and without shame, each of the girls picks up the large banana that has been resting on her lap. And puts it in her mouth.

Holy Mary, mother of God.

"Remember to relax your jaw . . . breathe on the outtake. Watch your teeth . . ."

My eyes are glued to Kate as the banana slides smoothly in and out from between her perfect pink lips. I'm so turned on, I could hammer nails into a two-by-four with my cock. I mean, I've been where that banana is going many times before, but something about watching Kate give head from this point of view is crazy erotic. It's like . . . live-porn dinner theater.

"Use your other hand, ladies. The testes are the neglected

stepchild of the male genitalia. Knead them, massage them, caress them—they need your love too."

Yes. Yes, they do.

In a hushed voice, Jack puts into words what all of us are thinking. "Anyone else about to jizz in their swim trunks? This is . . . this is like every fantasy I've ever had all rolled into one."

I can't help but agree. "Me too—except the part about my sister being there. And Delores."

Matthew is insulted. "Hey, my wife is magnificent."

You wanna know what else is magnificent? A black panther, streaking across a valley, going in for the kill. Doesn't mean I want to mount one.

I tear my eyes away from the fruit-blowing fest and look down at Matthew. "Your wife's a psychopath. I wouldn't fuck her with your dick. She'd probably pull some kind of booby-trap shit and shove razor blades up her twat to try and slice my cock off."

Was that too crude?

"That's a fucked-up thing to say."

Pick a conspiracy, any conspiracy—the JFK assassination, Area 51 . . .

"The truth usually is."

The guy code restricts how much you can mock a friend's significant other. There's an imaginary line. And if Matthew's reaction is any indication? I just crossed it.

He lands an angry punch to my right leg. In the spot above my knee—the charley-horse region—that makes pain echo up and down my femur.

"Ow! God damn it!"

I shift my weight to my other leg to keep from falling over, but I step on Warren's hand and set off a not-so-quiet domino effect.

"Hey! Those are my fingers, asshole!"

"Dude, stop pushing!"

"Shut the hell up, I can't hear!"

"You're ruining it!"

"Stop fucking punching me!"

You know what's going to happen next, don't you? Yep—the doors open. And the five of us tumble into the room in a heap—like a pileup after a fumble.

Of course.

There's a collective gasp at our intrusion—the kind of sound a sunbather would make after getting doused with a bucket of ice water. Meanwhile, the man-pile does its best to untangle.

"Ompf . . ."

"Ow . . ."

"Get your knee off my balls!"

"Get your balls off my knee!"

I'm the first to recover. I hop to my feet and flash the girls a dashing smile. "Hello, ladies." I hold up my hands, palms out. "Sorry for the interruption. Carry on, pretend like we're not even here."

But the lust spell has been broken. With a meaningful look, Delores peels her banana, then takes a big, chomping bite out of it.

I flinch.

My sister huffs, "You're back early."

Erin continues analyzing the remote control of the must-have vibrator. Kate is the only one who doesn't seem upset by our arrival. She leans back in her chair and stares at me dreamily, her dark eyes big and shiny. Then she sighs. "Hi, baby."

"Hey, sweetheart."

The rest of the guys are now standing, and Jack approaches dominatrix chick, who's busy packing up her naughty paraphernalia.

His come-on is a cross between James Bond and Rico Suave. "O'Shay. Jack O'Shay. If you're in need of an assistant or a model to demonstrate correct technique . . . I would be honored to fill that role. I'm available until tomorrow evening." He holds out his card and whispers, "Call me . . . cell phone's on the back."

She looks him up and down appreciatively, fingering the card with one red nail. "I'll keep your offer in mind."

But Matthew, like me, isn't ready for the party to end just yet. "Wait, you don't have to leave now."

Dee-Dee stands and holds up a magazine. "I have a catalog, Matthew. Let's look it over together in our room—you can make a Christmas list."

His eyes follow her as she walks out, then he scampers after her like a puppy chasing a bone.

Erin announces that she's taking a nap, and my sister and Steven disappear without a word to each other, or anyone else. My eyes never leave Kate. It's only been a few hours . . . but still . . . I missed her.

"You look relaxed," I comment. "Did you have a good afternoon?"

Kate stands and grazes her palms over my chest and across my shoulders, feeling me up. "It was nice. But I know how to make it even better." She wraps her arms around my neck and slides her tongue around my ear. It's soft at first—teasing. Then she plunges inside with the perfect amount of pressure to make my knees want to buckle.

Every guy has a spot. A highly sensitive place that, when stimulated, goes right to his dick. For some, it's the neck or the stomach. For some freaks it's the toes. But for me? It's my ears. Kate knows this.

Sucking lightly on my earlobe, her hands skim down my sides

around to the back, before settling on my ass with a firm squeeze. I'm not complaining—this is me here—a little grab-ass or jerk the johnson is never a bad thing. But Kate is usually more on the conservative side. Less overt with her sexual advances, particularly when other people are nearby.

I lean my head back to look at her face. Her smile is lazy, and her eyes—did I say they were shiny? They're not. They're *glassy.* There's a difference.

"Have you been smoking Warren's crotch stash?"

She bites her lip. Guilty as charged. She holds up two fingers, pinching them together, and closes one eye. "Just this much." Then she gives me an innocent, adorable look. "Are you mad?"

As I said before, I'm not into drugs. They're not just a vice—they're a crutch. A chemical support for weak-minded individuals who can't deal with life's everyday bullshit. But it's not like Kate is popping Mommy's Little Helpers three times a day. Since I've known her, she's gotten stoned exactly twice—both times with Dee-Dee, while the four of us were on vacation together. Kate doesn't buy or grow her own stuff. She would certainly never get high around our son.

So if she wants to kick back and toke up once in a blue moon, I'm not going to be the self-righteous, overbearing asshole who gives her shit for it. "Of course I'm not mad."

Her smile grows. "Oh . . . that's good. Because I have plans . . . plans that require you not being angry." She giggles wickedly. "Well . . . maybe a little angry would be okay."

Then she attaches her lips to my neck, sucking and kissing, moaning softly. Have I mentioned that weed makes Kate horny? Oh, yeah, it does. Which is another reason I'm perfectly happy with her current condition.

I sweep her up into my arms, princess style. She squeals. Then I tell Jack, "We'll be in our room. Don't knock on that door unless the place is on fucking fire."

Now that the goddess host has left the building, Jack's feeling needy. "I thought we were going to play Xbox?"

"Plans change." I swing around and make my way toward our room.

"That's not cool, man. Bros before . . ." My glare cuts him off. Because there's no way I'm going to let him finish that sentence when he's talking about my fiancée.

He takes the hint. "Fine. Dicks before chicks, then."

"You might want to rethink that. Because while you're out here jerking your game remote with Warren, I'm gonna be in there, with Kate. No contest, buddy."

I walk through our door and kick it closed behind me. Then I set Kate on her feet, cup her face with my hands, and kiss the breath right out of her. I pull the pink robe down her arm, exposing the creamy flesh of her shoulder. I taste it with my tongue, then slowly make my way up to her neck.

Her head rolls to the side with a moan. My hands make quick work of the robe and the black, strappy nightgown underneath—sliding them off Kate's body into a ring of satin around her feet. After kissing her lips deeply one last time, I kneel in front of her, soaking up the sight of her beautiful bareness.

She's perfect. It shouldn't surprise me—I know what she looks like. But still, every view of Kate's firm tits, her flat waist, her toned, smooth legs, revs me up like a kid getting his first glimpse of porn.

Because she's mine. Because she's amazing. Because she wants me as badly as I want her. And this is the way it's supposed to be—the way it's supposed to feel. The way it always will—an intense haze of lust and heat and adoration.

Her heavy-lidded eyes look down at me as I lean forward and kiss the skin around her pussy. She's completely smooth and soft—freshly waxed. Kate pulls back just a bit at the contact.

"Tender?" I ask.

It's times like this I'm particularly glad I'm a guy. Because manscaping with an electric razor is one thing. Getting hair ripped out in large clumps with hot wax? *No thanks*. Sounds like a goddamn torture technique, doesn't it?

Though the results are awesome.

She exhales. "Just a little sensitive."

"I'll be gentle."

I cup her ass and bring her sweet snatch to my mouth. I caress her with my tongue—like an artist stroking a fresh canvas. Slowly at first. Then deeper, with more purpose—more pressure. And I'm overwhelmed by the texture—the sight, the taste, and the scent. It's sublime sensory overload.

The saints can keep heaven, because this spot between Kate Brooks's legs is so much fucking better. Paradise on earth.

We'll stop right here for a second. Don't want to ruin the vibe—but we should talk about a "very special" topic. A topic that the male youth of today are tragically under-informed about. I like to call it cunning linguistics.

You may know it as going down. Dining at the Y. Carpet munching. Having a box lunch. The point is, pussy-eating is an acquired skill. All that making-the-alphabet-with-your-tongue crap is for lazy schmucks who couldn't find a G-spot with a fucking flashlight and a navigation device.

You have to hone your craft—develop your technique. It's a lot like . . . basketball. Just knowing the right moves isn't a guarantee you're gonna score points. Because you have to know whom you're playing with—the type of moves they're partial to. Too much attention to a sensitive clit kills the momentum. Not enough attention and the chick will be checking her watch thinking, *Is he done yet?* Body language is crucial. Reading the signals—taking cues.

At the moment, Kate's pussy is dripping—wet desire clings to her thighs. And it's fucking glorious. Women should never be embarrassed about being turned on. Even if you squirt like a high-powered water gun or gush like Old Reliable—be proud. Guys love it.

Because it can't be faked.

As "Sally" demonstrated in that 1980s Billy Crystal movie, just because a woman acts as if she were coming, it doesn't mean she really is. For some, every pant, scratch, and squeal may be suspect. Is she really getting off? Or is she just tired of getting nailed? But feeling, seeing, that slick desire tells men that you're actually into it. That *they're* doing it *right*. And that makes us guys want to do it *more*.

Now that my good deed is done for the day—back to the bedroom.

Kate's hips start to rotate against my face. My hands help her along. She leans her upper body back against the wall. Her breaths come faster and her face turns upward. Her eyes close. Then the explosion comes. She grabs the back of my head, holding me in place as she clenches and grinds against me. Her mouth opens, but no sound comes out.

Fucking gorgeous.

After a minute, her grip loosens, and her eyes open. She looks down at me with a satisfied smile, and I kiss a path up her body as I stand. Her limp arms rise slowly up and around my neck, and just before she presses her mouth to mine, she whispers, "So good."

I thought so too, but it's always nice to hear. As she kisses me, my hands find her ass again. Kate's ass reminds me of a kid's favorite stuffed animal. Once it's within my reach, I just can't seem to let it go.

I drag her up my body and her legs lock around my waist. Now that I've gotten Kate off, my plan is to slow things down. Take our time. Because once you have kids—time is never your friend again. Even in the dead of night, there's always the thought, the nagging fucking possibility, that time will run out. But that's not the case now.

James—whom I love with everything I am—is my parents' problem. I plan to make the most of it. By spending the next few hours doing all the fun, naughty—*loud*—things I wouldn't risk doing when he's nearby.

"I owe you a massage," I whisper to her.

But Kate has other ideas. She reaches down between us and pulls my rock-hard dick out of my swim shorts. She strokes it expertly, until my eyes cross. "You can massage me later. I need you to fuck me right now."

Christ. I love it when she gets bossy. With one hand, I push my shorts down the rest of the way. Then I line us up and slide slowly inside. "God *damn.*" Her body swells around me. Takes me in and holds me tight.

It might sound stupid—overly romantic—to say that Kate's body was made for mine. But that doesn't make it any less true. My hips pull back, and her muscles squeeze harder, not wanting to let me go. I push in deeper till Kate's ass hits the wall behind her. I pump into her with short, hard strokes, thumping against the wall in a drumming rhythm. We gasp and moan together—cursing and humming—with every thrust.

It's not gentle. Or quiet. We're loud enough for the rest of the house to hear us. Hell, we're loud enough for Indonesia to hear us. Holding her against me, I turn around so my back's braced against the doorframe of the bathroom. I lift her up and down smoothly. My arms strain from the action, and a sheen of sweat covers our skins.

Then I take a few steps into the bathroom, to the vanity counter. I perch her on top, knocking clinking bottles of perfume and face wash to the floor. I kiss her deeply, and her tongue dances against mine. She pulls back and grips my hips with her hands, taking over the pace.

She moans and begs and orders, "Slow."

I do as she commands, rotating my hips in sensuously slow circles. Clashing against her, bringing us closer to that powerful pinnacle with every breath we take.

"Fuck . . . ," I hiss, because it feels too good not to.

"Drew . . . ," she answers with a soulful whimper.

Kate's legs tremble, shake under my steady hands. I move faster, pump against her harder, greedy for the feeling of her tight, hot muscles pulsing and contracting around me. The heels of the black shoes that still encase her feet dig into my ass as she matches the give-and-take of my hips with her own.

Then she's clinging to me—chest to chest—her teeth biting into my shoulder as she screams. "Yes . . . yes . . ."

When you've had as many orgasms as I have, they tend to blend together, forming one general happy memory. But every once in a while, one stands out from the rest. It's a moment I'll think about later—relive on my next business trip when masturbation is my only recourse.

This is one of those orgasms.

Ecstasy rips through me like a submarine missile tearing into the ocean. I lean forward over Kate, pressing her against me. Trying to get closer—to absorb every ounce of bliss she's giving me. I think I shout her name, but I'm not sure.

Several moments later, after the sound of my blood pounding in my ears has lessened, I look into Kate's smiling eyes. She pushes my damp hair off my forehead. Then she kisses the tattoo of our son's name on my chest.

And she hugs me—holds me—resting her cheek against my heart. "I love you, Drew."

It should be weird to have such sweet words and tender actions come after the rough and raw screwing we just enjoyed. But for us? Nothing weird about it.

For us, it's perfect.

Chapter 9

I did eventually give Kate that massage. Not that she needed it, relaxed as she was—but rubbing warm baby oil on Kate's body is my idea of a really good time. It doesn't take a genius to figure out how things went from there. Which is why, at the moment, Kate is passed out cold on the bed. I'll let her sleep another twenty minutes or so before I'll have to wake her. Because it's common knowledge that women take forever and a day to get ready for a night on the town. Kate may be different from most girls in a lot of ways—but in that way? She's exactly the same.

I walk out of the bedroom to the kitchen, looking for some nourishment. Man can't live on sex alone—as cool an idea as that would be. The house is quiet. Jack and Warren probably took off to escape the sounds of bumping and grinding all around them.

I make myself a turkey on rye in the kitchen, then I glance out the balcony doors and spot my sister. Sitting alone on the private brick patio in the rear of the villa.

Mentally I shake my head and step out through the doors.

Alexandra glances at me quickly, then turns her eyes back to the foliage surrounding the yard. Forlorn is not a look I'm used to seeing on my sister. It's unsettling.

I sit down in the lawn chair beside her and put my sandwich on the table. I should start off kindly. Unaccusing. Considerate. I should be diplomatic.

"What the fuck, Lexi?"

She takes a sip from the martini glass in her hand before placing it on the table. "Go away, Drew. I'd like to be alone."

"I'd like to buy a private island in the South Pacific and name it Drewland, but that's not going to happen anytime soon. We can't always have what we want."

I pick up the pink-concoction-filled glass and give it a sniff. My head jerks back and my nose wrinkles. Whatever my sister's been drinking smells like fruity ammonia—like strawberry-scented bat piss.

"If you're going to poison your body, at least have the decency to use a premium-brand toxin." Cheap liquor is strictly reserved for winos and college kids who don't know any better.

Her face is impassive. Slack and sad. She shakes her head slightly. "You don't understand."

I toss her drink onto the grass. "I resent that. I'll have you know I understand all perspectives—man, woman, or child. God and I are a lot alike that way." I pause for a second and my voice softens. "What's wrong, Alexandra? Whatever it is, maybe I can help."

Her tone is flat. Lifeless. "Steven is going to divorce me."

I snort. "With the way you've been acting lately, I don't blame him."

I ready my hand to block the glass that I'm pretty certain is about to come spiraling at my face. But nothing gets thrown at me. Instead something more shocking—more horrifying—happens.

The Bitch covers her face with her hands and sobs into them.

I swallow hard. Then I look around. Waiting for that douche bag Ashton Kutcher to jump out and yell, "Punked!" Because Alexandra Evans isn't a crier. She's a doer—a fixer.

And throughout the history of mankind, crying has never fixed shit.

I stutter. And ask the second-stupidest question ever. "Are you . . . are you crying?"

In my head Tom Hanks's voice echoes, *"There's no crying in baseball!"* Did Cleopatra cry when Egypt got sacked? Did Joan of Arc cry when the Catholic Church called her a witch? They are my sister's counterparts.

Alexandra shakes her head, but the tears keep on flowing. "It's my fault. I've pushed him away. I've been miserable to be around. I've treated him terribly."

"Well, if you know that, why don't you just . . . stop?" Seems simple, right?

Wrong.

"I can't help it. I'm so sad. And angry. It's not fair. I'm too young to be a dried-up prune!"

Now she's really going at it. Sniffling and snotting all over the place. I don't have a tissue, so I take off my T-shirt—even though it's one of my favorites—and hand it to her. Alexandra blows her nose into it. It sounds like a dying goose.

Even though I have no fucking clue what she's talking about, I know I'm supposed to say something. "Well . . . prunes have their uses. A few months ago, James's pipes were backed up. And we fed him a few of those bad boys and they did the trick. It was like edible Drano—cleaned everything out. Prunes are great."

She stops. And looks up at me with red-rimmed, perplexed eyes. "What the hell are you talking about?"

"I have no fucking idea! I'm trying to be comforting."

"Well, it's a good thing I don't come to you for comfort often. You suck at it!" She goes back to bawling in the T-shirt.

I pinch the bridge of my nose and breathe deep. Let's try this again. "You said you were angry. Sad. Why are you angry and sad, Alexandra?"

She wipes at her face and talks quickly—rushed. "I could set my watch to my period. Every twenty-seven days on the dot. So when it didn't come, I thought, *Oh, crap,* you know? And even though the test said negative, I assumed it was just too early. So I went to the doctor and I was so sure he was going to tell me I was pregnant. And even though it wasn't planned, I started to get used to the idea of another one. I was excited. But then . . . then he told me I wasn't pregnant."

A cold ball of ice settles in my stomach. "You're not . . . you're not sick, are you?"

She shakes her head. "No. I'm not sick." She takes a cleansing breath. "He said it's menopause. Early-onset menopause. I can't have any more children—ever. I'm infertile."

She weeps quietly for a minute.

I rub her shoulder gently. "Did you and Steven want a lot more kids?"

Her brow furrows slightly. "Well . . . no. We'd always planned on two. After Thomas was born, I'd even talked to Steven about getting a vasectomy. He wasn't keen on the idea."

I try to understand the problem. That fails, so I ask, "But, if you don't want any more kids—then why are you so devastated about not being able to have any more kids?"

"Because I'm a woman, Drew! Creating life. Nurturing—that's what we do."

Nope—still don't get it. "But that's not *all* you do. I mean,

Jesus, Alexandra, it's not like you're a *Handmaid's Tale* breeder here. So the egg basket's empty? Big deal. You have two beautiful children—be happy with them. Maybe this is nature's way of telling you that you shouldn't have any more. I've seen what pregnancy does to your body. It ain't pretty."

Now she's glaring at me. Which is a good sign. Pissed-off Alexandra I can handle.

"I *am* happy with the two that I have. It's just . . . having the option to have more was nice . . . even if I never did. I feel . . . cheated. And old. I have the insides of a sixty-year-old woman, Drew. How long before the outside reflects that? And have you looked at Steven lately? Every year he gets more handsome—more distinguished looking. Soon some gold-digging bimbo is going to try to get her claws in him, and he's going to be saddled with a wife who looks like Barbara Bush!"

She buries her face in the shirt again, and I can't help but laugh. Just a little. "Lexi . . . you're hardly Barbara Bush. I'd say you're more of the Christie Brinkley variety. And besides—Steven loves you. *You.* Not your goddamn ovaries. You're the bitchy-boss center of his universe. You always have been. When the rest of us were jerking off to thoughts of Sister B, Steven was jerking off to thoughts of you." And don't think I'm comfortable knowing that. "He'd never trade you in for some skinny-legged twit who's only interested in the size of his bank account. Steven is too smart for that."

She looks up. Almost hopefully. "How would you feel if Kate told you she couldn't have any more kids?"

I take a moment to ponder. To imagine the possibilities. "If Kate told me I could bang her all I wanted and I never had to worry about knocking her up? I'd do the Irish jig down Fifth fucking Avenue. It'd be like Christmas every day. No more PMS, no more abstaining for three to five days every month . . . unless you let Steven go wading in the crimson tide? Which, if you do, please lie to me."

Period sex is a deal breaker for Kate. No matter what I say, no matter what I do, she's not interested. Which I will *never* understand. We're hunters, ladies. We *like* blood. It's part of the reason action flicks and war movies have so much of it. We don't think it's gross. We don't think it's messy. It's just . . . more lubrication.

Don't look at me like that. I'm just being honest.

The tears have almost dried up. Alexandra sniffles and hiccups. "But don't you want more children?"

"Sure, I want more. James is the best. I'd have twenty with Kate. In *theory*. Reality's a different story. Kids are hard."

Alexandra nods.

"You need to talk to Steven. You're torturing the guy. It's cruel and unusual punishment."

"What if he looks at me differently?"

"He won't."

"How can you be sure?"

I lean forward and try to find the right words. "Because . . . because when Kate was pregnant with James? She was as big as a house—and I still wanted to fuck her every bit as much as I want to right now. Because when I look at her? I just see Kate . . . the woman who walked into my life five years ago and screwed it all up. Who shook me out, turned me upside down, and made me . . . more. So even when she gets wrinkly or gray? She'll still be Kate. She'll still make me laugh and make me crazy . . . and she'll still love me more than I will ever deserve. And I know that Steven feels the same way about you."

Alexandra wipes her eyes with my shirt one last time. She starts to look more like herself. "So . . . you're saying I'm making a bigger deal about this than it is?"

"I'm saying if you tell Steven, it won't feel so big anymore."

She gives me a small smile. "You're right. I know you're right. I'll talk to him tonight."

"Good."

Alexandra stands up, leans in, and hugs me. I squeeze her back, letting her know that I'm here for her. To listen, and to kick her in the ass whenever the rare opportunity presents itself.

"And don't go making a habit out of this falling-apart thing," I chastise. "I have an exclusive on self-destructive behavior in this family."

She chuckles and heads toward the house. Then she pauses and turns toward me. "Hey, Drew?"

"Yeah?"

"When did you get so smart?"

That's an easy one. "About five years ago."

After I finish my sandwich, I head back to the bedroom to wake Kate. But when I get there, she's already up and in the shower. Washing the body I obsess about and singing.

Nobody does it half as good as you
Baby, you're the best

Her voice floats around the bathroom and echoes off the tiles. It's a cheesy song—Carly Simon—from some seventies James Bond flick. But pleasure still rises up from my gut and spreads out through my chest at the sound. Because as sure as I know Delores will one day be committed to a home for the criminally insane, I know Kate is singing about me. I fold my arms, lean back against the door, and watch her through the steamed glass. She tilts her head back under the hot stream of water. Her rack juts out high and proud—more tantalizing than any Vegas showgirl's set. Her long hair brushes against her ass, playing peekaboo with the butterfly tattoo on her lower back.

Kate turns off the water and steps out of the shower. She smiles when she sees me. "Hey, you. Where'd you go?"

I should probably hand her a towel. It would be the nice thing to do. The bathroom tiles are cool, and if her pointy nipples are any indication, she's a bit chilled. But you don't really think I'm going to do that, do you?

Come on.

Like I would ever pass up the chance to eyefuck Kate Brooks in all her wet, bare-ass beauty. And pointy nipples are awesome. So, like the giggly, perverted schoolboy part of me still is, I don't move an inch as Kate scurries across the bathroom and grabs a robe off the hook on the far wall, then covers up my favorite viewing pleasure.

"I was on the patio with Alexandra."

Kate twists a second towel around her head in that high-crown style that only women are capable of. Then she frowns worriedly. "She really hasn't been herself lately. I hope she'll talk to me tonight about whatever's going on between her and Steven."

"Way ahead of you. It's all taken care of."

"What's happened?"

I reach into the shower and turn the water back on full blast. Then I slip off my boxers. Despite the seriousness of the conversation, Kate does a little eyefucking of her own.

Nice.

"Her baby-making factory got an early foreclosure notice."

"What does that mean?"

"Doctor told her she's menopausal."

Kate's hand goes to her chest with a sympathetic sigh. "But she's so young!"

I nod. "Yeah. She's a hot mess about it. She's been afraid to tell Steven, but I convinced her to talk to him later. They'll get back on track."

Kate's eyes widen. "*You* convinced her to talk to Steven?"

"Yep."

"How did you manage that?"

"She talked, bawled her eyes out, and I . . . comforted . . . her."

Now Kate looks confused. "You *comforted* her?"

"What are you, a fucking parrot? Yes, I comforted her—why are you shocked?"

Kate folds her arms across her chest. "Well, let's see. Could it be because your idea of comforting Mackenzie when her cat died was to tell her not to be sad because now Snowball was with all his other feline friends in hell?"

I possibly could have worded that better.

"Or maybe it's because when my mother missed James's christening because of that blizzard, you *comforted* her by saying that when he grows up, he'll barely know who she is anyway?"

Some people just can't handle the truth.

"Then there was the time—"

I put my hand over her smart-ass mouth. Her dark, deep eyes stare up at me with warmth and teasing affection.

"I admit, not everyone is able to absorb my particular brand of comfort. But in this case, Alexandra did. Because of me, she and Steven are on their way back to marital bliss. For that, I deserve a pat on the back. A hand job would also do nicely."

Kate busts out laughing. She wraps her arms around my neck,

pressing her terry-cloth-covered stomach against my dick. She tilts her head up. "It's nice to be the stable couple in the group for once. Go, us." She holds up one palm. "High five."

I glance at her hand, then shake my head dismissively. "I don't do high fives." I wiggle my digits. "But if you're interested in some fingering, I'm happy to oblige."

Kate giggles. "Such a pervert."

I give her lips a peck. "For you? Always. Now stop trying to seduce me, and let me take a shower."

As she turns away, I swat her ass for good measure. Then I step into the shower and close the glass door behind me. I stick my head under the searing water and let the heat relax the muscles in my neck and back.

Through the glass a blurry Kate moves around, beginning the long getting-ready ritual. "I called your parents to see how the baby was doing."

"What'd they say?"

"Your mother sounded half-dead, but all of the kids are great."

Just as I expected.

Five minutes later, I'm out of the shower. I towel off and slip on a fresh pair of boxers. Then I step up to the sink and lather shaving cream on my face. Kate reenters the bathroom and stands beside me, putting makeup on. Her hair is damp but the robe is gone. In its place is a mouthwatering matching bra-and-panty set.

They're pink silk with a black lace overlay. The panties are high cut—bikini style—and the bra pushes her tits up and together, creating a sexy-as-all-hell deep cleavage line. She dusts powder onto her face while I check her out.

"New underwear?" I keep a mental catalog of all of Kate's undergarments, organized by color and style. I've never seen these before. I definitely would've remembered them.

She turns her hips, showing me the goods. "Yeah, aren't they cute?"

Cute? No. Boner inducing? Definitely.

"There's a La Perla boutique downstairs. I bought them before our spa treatments."

I can't help but contemplate what she was thinking when she bought them. I mean, a steamy night at home after James is asleep is one thing—a new outfit always makes that more interesting. But tonight we won't even be hanging out together. Depending on what condition we're in when we make it back to the room, we'll be lucky if we even pass out next to each other.

"Huh."

That one syllable gives her pause. The hand that was applying eyeliner stops and she looks at me. "What?"

I keep shaving. "You don't have any . . . other . . . underwear with you?"

Her brow wrinkles. "Sure I do. You don't like these?"

I rinse my razor in the sink. "No . . . they're fine. I just thought maybe you could wear something different. Something whiter, cotton, more full coverage."

A triple-locked chastity belt would also suffice.

Her head tilts, trying to figure out where I'm going with this. "No, Drew, I didn't bring any granny panties with me."

You think I'm crazy, I know. But I'm not. I told you a long time ago—I play chess. I don't just think about the next move; I think about the move five moves from now. So I can't help but question why the hell would Kate buy new panties that would make any man with half a pulse want to sink to his knees in front of her and shred them with his teeth? It's like . . . when a woman shaves her legs before a first date, even if she's wearing pants. Maybe she doesn't realize it, maybe she doesn't want to admit it—but the only reason she's doing it is because some part of her brain is hoping she'll get laid.

"Huh."

Kate just looks sideways at me. I pat my chin with a hand towel while she finishes her makeup. As she smooths gloss over her succulent lips, I can't help but speak up.

"Flavored lip gloss, huh?"

"Okay, that's it." She puts the cap on the gloss with a snap and drops it in her bag. Then she turns toward me quickly. "You need to stop. Right now."

"Stop what? I didn't say anything."

"You didn't have to. I know what's going on in that deviant head of yours."

I cross my arms. "You think so?"

"I *know* so. You're having this whole conversation with yourself about why I would buy new underwear and who I'm going to let see it. Then you're thinking, why am I putting on flavored lip gloss? Why not just *plain* lip gloss—unless I want someone to taste it?"

God, she's good.

"But the truth is, I bought the underwear for *me*. Because having bras and underwear that match make me feel more put together. And you should know, Mr. I See Everything, that the flavored lip gloss is the only gloss I use. Every day."

"You sound awfully defensive, Kate."

"This isn't defensive. This is a natural reaction to having to deal with the twisted way you view the world."

We stare at each other for a few seconds, arms crossed, not giving an inch. Until Kate does. She plucks a tissue from the box on the back of the toilet and wipes the gloss off her lips. With a ring of sarcasm in her tone she asks, "There. Happy now?"

I should be. I mean—I won, right? But it's kind of hard to be happy when you're acting like a douche.

"And since the underwear concerns you so much"—she slides the scrap of silk and lace down her legs and tosses it to me—"I won't wear any."

She moves to exit the bathroom, but I step in front of her. "Whoa! Wait up—let's pause the crazy talk for a second."

I hold Kate's gaze for a few seconds. Then—thoroughly contrite—I sink to my knees in front of her.

Her arms are still folded, but her eyes soften. Kate likes me on my knees.

"Your point is well taken."

Her eyebrows rise in feigned innocence. "What point is that?"

I smile. "That I should trust you. That I do trust you." I pick up one foot and kiss her light-pink-painted toes, before sliding it through the leg of the underwear. Kate drops her arms, using my shoulders for balance, as I repeat the action with the other foot. I slide the panties up her legs, kissing each thigh reverently as I go. "Every flavored-lip-gloss-slathered, fuck-hot-panty-covered inch of you, I trust."

She smiles forgivingly as I retrieve the gloss and replace it on those flawless lips. She rubs them together, then she sighs. "I already told you this bachelorette-party thing is not worth it if it's going to cause problems between us. Be honest if you can't handle it. Do you want me to tell Delores to call tonight off?"

Doesn't *that* just make me feel like the biggest insecure pussy that ever walked the face of the earth? But we should examine this moment more closely for a second. Because in life, we make choices—ones that seem completely harmless and totally insignificant.

Until they play out.

Only in hindsight do we realize the monumental effect our decisions have. It's the businessman who decides to go in to work a few minutes late and misses a fatal collision by seconds. The teenager who chooses to hold a grudge against her mother, and it turns out to be the last conversation they ever have. The guy on the street who finds a dollar and uses it to buy a winning lottery ticket.

Small choices can lead to huge consequences.

I was trying to be unselfish. I wanted to do the right thing.

You can bet your ass I won't be making *that* mistake again.

"No one's calling anything off," I say confidently. "I had a jealous-dickhead seizure—completely temporary. The green-eyed monster will stay in his cage the rest of the weekend. The *one*-eyed monster will want to play with you later on."

She laughs and takes my face in her hands. "My panties are for your eyes only."

"I know."

Kate stretches up and kisses me. And I taste strawberry. "You're going to go out with the guys and be assaulted by money-hungry strippers—and I'm okay with that."

I nod. "And you're going to go out with the girls and be surrounded by horny, half-naked men—and it won't bother me."

"We're the stable couple in the group now."

"We'll have a good time—no problems."

When I told her that? I honestly believed it.

Chapter 10

Some men wear expensive suits because they want to feel as if they have money, even if they don't. Others wear them because they want to show people how much money they have. For me, it's all about the mind-set. The attitude. I've never had a problem with confidence, but for guys who do, a custom-fitted suit makes you walk taller, stand straighter. It makes your balls bigger and gives off that *GoodFellas,* don't-fuck-with-me kind of vibe.

I unbutton the jacket of my charcoal Ermenegildo Zegna and pour myself three fingers of Scotch from the wet bar in the living room. Jack, Matthew, and Steven share my affinity for a well-made suit and are decked out in their own Gucci, Newman, and Armani respectively. Our stud quotient is high—any female within a twenty-foot radius is bound to get caught in our tractor beam.

Then Warren walks out of his room. Wearing a wrinkled green T-shirt, tan carpenter shorts, and sandals. Yes—frigging sandals.

I take a sip of my drink and stare at him. "If I'd known we were going to the skate park, I would've brought my board."

He's perplexed. Then he looks at the rest of us and back at his own attire. He shrugs. "I like to be comfortable. You guys look like you're going to a funeral. I look relaxed."

"You look like a loser," I argue. "And that's unacceptable for tonight. My guidance will only get you so far. If you wanna attract quality snatch? You need to step up your game. That means a half-decent suit, or at least a pair of pressed slacks—preferably ones not made from the same material as prison jumpsuits." I toss back the rest of my drink. "And what the hell is with your hair?"

Warren's wavy, light brown locks are less tamed than usual. They're higher—poofier—like an old lady fresh from the hairdresser. He pats the top of his head self-consciously. "I forgot my gel. But it's cool—chicks dig the curls."

"Yeah, if it's 1998 and your name is Justin Timberlake."

Jack intervenes. "I'll hook you up, dude. I always bring my buzzer along. We'll trim the mop-top, slick it back—your own mother won't recognize you."

Steven sets his Scotch down on a coaster. Then he taps his chin thoughtfully. "And I'll call the concierge—have them send over something from the Armani boutique near the lobby." He eyes Warren up and down. "You're a thirty, maybe a thirty-two waist, with a slim-cut jacket. A light blue tie will really bring out the color of your eyes."

Welcome, ladies and gentlemen, to another edition of *Queer Eye for the Straight Guy*.

And Matthew makes it so much worse. He claps his fingertips together daintily and says in a high-pitched voice, "Makeover time!"

My eyes narrow in his direction. "Don't ever do that again."

"Too much?"

"Definitely."

Twenty minutes later Warren is decked out in a slick navy suit, black shirt, and shiny Prada shoes. His hair has a neat wet look—short on top, combed back at the sides. He looks . . . passable. Extremely awkward and uncomfortable—but passable.

I stand in front of him and brush off his shoulders, inspecting his clothes like a general at boot camp.

While he whines like a bitch. "It itches." He rolls his neck and steps from one foot to the other.

"Stop fucking fidgeting."

He pulls at the collar. "It's stiff."

"It's new—it's supposed to be. Stand up straight." *Jesus*, do I sound like my father or what?

I drape the blue tie around his neck, to demonstrate how to tie one. But then I think better of it.

There's an excellent chance I'll end up strangling him with the damn thing. And a trip out to the desert to bury a body would be a major inconvenience right now.

Steven, who has turned patience into an art form, takes my place. "Okay, Billy, the rabbit comes out of his burrow, goes around the tree . . ."

You can tell a lot about a person by the game he or she plays at a casino. Adrenaline junkies, those willing to take big risks for an even bigger payoff, they orbit the craps tables. Craps is a game of skillful luck. It requires a certain finesse—quick thinking and decisive action. Then there's blackjack. Unless you're a freak-of-nature card counter, you have to stick to the rules. Assume each card's a ten, stay at fifteen even if every fiber of your being is screaming to hit, and wait for the dealer to bust. If you don't know how to play, stay the fuck away. Blackjackers tend to throw quite the hissy fit if you take "their" card. After blackjack, there's roulette. Roulette is all about odds. Play black or red and you have a slightly less than 50 percent chance of winning. Statistically speaking, it's your best shot at beating the house.

At the low end of the gambling totem pole are the slot machines. A monkey could play them. Put your money in, pull the lever; money, lever; money, lever. They require no proficiency or knowledge and they're programmed to favor the casino. The longer you play, the more likely you are to go broke.

The only people who play slots are the aged, the mentally infirm, and suckers.

"Cool—slot machines! That's all I play. I'm so good at them," Warren says.

Saw that one coming a mile away, didn't you?

I slap him on the back and steer him toward the high-roller section. "Tonight you're gonna play craps."

"I don't know how to play craps."

"Then you're going to watch and learn. Craps is a man's game. All the hottest girls hang out at the craps table because that's where the money is. If the mountain won't come to Muhammad, than he has to go to the motherfucking mountain."

"What mountain?"

For a second I forgot I was talking to a real, live sphincter. "Never mind. Just pay attention."

Matthew, Warren, and I get our chips while Jack heads over to blackjack. Steven gets comfortable at a $5,000-minimum roulette table. He's all about statistics and odds. At the craps table, I'm rolling and Matthew handles the bets. Right out of the gate, I roll a seven, and the crowd goes wild.

Matthew pounds my back excitedly. "Yes! Mickey fucking Mantle! Keep 'em coming!"

Fifteen minutes later, we've tripled our money. The number of bystanders around the table has doubled. Warren still has no idea how to play the game, but he takes his cues from the crowd and responds accordingly. Everyone is laughing, drinking, elbowing in to place money on the table—trying to get a piece of the action. It's wild. Fun. It feels like the old days—just me and the boys out for a good time. There are no worries about kids or weddings, no stress about work or any of the bullshit that real life abounds in.

Then real life taps me on the shoulder.

Dice in hand, I turn around. And come face-to-face with the dark-haired, blue-eyed flight attendant from the airplane. She's wearing a black, strapless cocktail dress and heels high enough to put her at eye level with me. She's not alone. In triangle formation behind her are two equally attractive women. One is blond and baby faced, shorter, with fuller curves. The other is a brunette with blond streaks, olive skin, and full, ripe lips.

Blue-Eyes smiles wide. "Hello again."

I don't want to be rude, but—screw it—I'll go with rude. "What are you doing here?"

"You said this was where you were staying."

"I also said we'd be busy."

She responds coyly, "But I saw the look you gave me. I knew you only said that so your girlfriend wouldn't get upset. So she wouldn't think you were interested."

Okay—I'm all for women who are assertive. You are sexual

beings with needs. Own it. Relish it. But coming on strong to a guy who blatantly doesn't want you isn't going to change his mind.

It just makes you look pathetic.

Her hand reaches out to rub my chest, but I catch her wrist before she makes contact.

"Except I'm really *not* interested."

Like a horny ghost, Jack appears at my side. "I, on the other hand, am *very* interested." He takes her elbow and leads her away. "Don't mind Drew—he's a blind fool. How about we get you a drink?"

The brunette friend fades into the crowd, but the baby face just stands there looking blank. She twirls her hair in that "dumb blonde" way that makes me suspect her IQ may actually be lower than Warren's. But she's hot—definitely a step above the trough he's been feeding at lately. I nudge him with my arm and jerk my chin in the blonde's direction.

He wipes his hands on his pants nervously. Then he speaks to her. "Hey, wanna hear a joke?"

And all my hard work goes down the fucking tubes.

"Okay," she answers.

"What did the blanket say when it fell off the bed?"

"What?"

"Oh, sheet."

Blondie's lips pout in confusion. "I don't get it. Is the blanket, like, computerized?"

Warren's face falls. "No . . . it's . . . let me try another one. What did the duck say . . ."

I wrap my arm around his neck and squeeze, cutting off his air supply just a little. "Billy—remember what the doctor said about your voice?"

I turn to the girl, hoping to salvage Operation PPFW. That's Premium Pussy for Warren, in case you weren't sure.

"My friend here is a singer. Billy Warren? He has to save his voice for his next concert—doctor's orders."

Her eyes open wide and her tone is dim-witted. "My horoscope said I was going to meet someone famous today! Billy Warren—I didn't recognize you. I totes loved your last single."

Matthew calls, "Drew, come on—you gotta roll."

"Right." I fish a handful of quarters from my pocket and slap them into Warren's hands. "Why don't you kids go play the slots? You'll be safer there."

With a giggle, Blondie informs me, "The way the wheels go around and around is so funny! I love slot machines."

"That makes so much sense," I tell her.

Could you imagine the children these two would have? Maybe genetic selection isn't evil after all.

I shove Warren away. "And remember, don't fucking talk. *At all.*"

He smiles and gives me two thumbs up. He looks so grateful and brainless, I can't help but laugh as they walk away.

Twenty minutes later, Matthew and I are still on fire. Unstoppable. He's taken over rolling, and I shift our chips around, betting big because we're up by a lot. Matthew rolls a two and the room erupts in cheers. I give him a man shake and double our bet.

Which is when a certain semi-stalker flight attendant shows up next to me. Again.

"Can I give you a blow?"

My ears immediately perk up. "Excuse me?"

She points to Matthew. "The dice. Can I blow them for you? For luck?"

How about you blow me instead? I immediately think. Because I may be a man in a committed relationship—but I'm still a man.

That is the curse of evolution. Instincts. It's why most guys have such a hard time with monogamy. Because our natural drive is to spread our seed around—offer it to as many willing partners as possible. We don't have to act on it, but the impulse is always there. So the next time you think your guy is flirting with some random ho bag? Try not to get too upset. He's waging an epic internal battle against his own body's inclinations.

"Not needed," I tell her. "We're on a streak—never mess with a streak. These dice are doing fine on their own."

My phone buzzes in my pocket. The text from Kate says the girls are finally ready and on their way down to the casino.

Flight girl leans over my shoulder and looks at my phone. "Cute kid. He yours?"

She's referring to the picture of James on my main screen. I took it a few weeks ago, when I was trying to get James to eat a bowl of pasta. He wasn't pleased with his meal and told me so by dumping the whole fucking thing on his head.

"Yep."

She moves close to my ear and cuts me off. "We don't have to play these games. I have a hotel room waiting two blocks away. I want you. It's obvious you want me. Stop fighting it."

I lean back. "Did we forget to take our meds this morning?"

She laughs. Sounds kind of like Norman Bates, doesn't she? Throughout my debauched pre-Kate years, I encountered my fair share of *Fatal Attraction*, I'll-never-fuck-you-even-if-you-are-that-hot-because-you-obviously-have-several-screws-loose women. They're out there and they're not hard to spot. I was a master at avoiding, deflecting, and escaping their fanatical grasp.

But it looks as if I'm out of practice. Because before I can stop her, she swipes the phone out of my hand and moves back a few steps.

Anger flashes on my face and in my voice. "Give me back my goddamn phone."

She smiles. "Come and get it." She puts my phone down her frigging dress.

You have *got* to be kidding me. I turn to Matthew. "I don't suppose you want to help me out with this?"

He looks down at the chips, then back to me. "There's like a hundred grand here, man."

Of course there is.

Have you ever seen *Flash Gordon*? You know that scene where Flash has to put his hand in the rock? The one with the grotesque, prickly snake thing inside it, just waiting to bite him? That's pretty much what I'm feeling right now.

I crack my knuckles and shake my hands out. "Cover me. I'm going in." Then I shove my hand down the front of her dress. I limit the physical contact as best I can, but the dress is tight. So upon entry, I immediately realize this chick is sporting a fake set of tits. And a nipple ring.

Don't judge me. Do I look like I'm enjoying this, for God's sake?

Psycho Flight Girl, on the other hand, seems to be enjoying it a whole bunch, if her moans are any indication. "Oooh, that's nice. A little to the left."

I roll my eyes and try to find a happy place. Then, the most improbable thing happens. Or, an absolute certainty, depending on your point of view.

"What the *hell* is this?!"

Care to guess whose voice that is?

I don't even have to turn around, but I do. "Kate!"

I shake my head, trying my damnedest to deny that any of this is happening. "This isn't . . . I'm not . . ." Yes, my arm is still biceps deep inside this chick's dress.

I rip it out.

And point at her like an older sister accusing a younger one of wearing her favorite sweater. "She took my phone and won't give it back."

Sensing I'm in deep shit, Warren and Jack wander over to watch the show. Matthew just keeps gambling.

Kate struts forward and holds out her hand, simultaneously subjecting the woman to the thousand-watt bitch-glare.

The psycho woman rolls her eyes and takes the phone out of her dress. Kate gets an ever-ready bottle of antibacterial spray out of her purse, squirts the phone with it, wipes it with a tissue, then hands it back to me—spraying my hand for good measure.

After that, all of Kate's pissed-off radiance turns back to the flight attendant. Her voice is low and deadly serious. "I put up with your shit on the plane because I didn't want to spend the first hours of my vacation in the custody of federal air marshals. But we're not on the plane now." Kate holds up her left hand. "See this ring? It means I belong to him. And the tattoo of my name on his arm means he belongs to me. *All* of him. His dick is a compass, and I'm due north—it *only* points to me."

Well, there's something you don't hear every day.

"So you are going to disappear, right now. Or I'm going to kick your ass from one end of this casino to the other. And you might want to take a look around—'cause it's a damn big casino."

The flight attendant's eyes narrow into slits. As she replies, her head does that urban-slide thing that looks incredibly fucking stupid but means she's ready for war. "You think you can take me? You and what army, bitch?"

Erin walks up and stands next to Kate. "This one."

Psycho laughs—and I kind of don't blame her. Even in heels, Erin is shorter than Kate by about two inches. Together, they're not exactly poster girls for intimidation. Until Dee-Dee comes on the scene. And although her physical stature isn't that different from Erin's and Kate's, the disturbed, unbalanced look in her eyes makes up for it in a big way.

I shiver.

Psycho Woman stands her ground, but her expression is a little less sure. Then comes the icing on the cake. Which would be my sister—standing a foot above the other girls like the mighty Amazon she is.

Her smile is downright scary. "The way my hormones are raging, I would like nothing more than to rip out those cheap extensions on your head and nail them to my wall like a hunting trophy."

Now Psycho actually looks frightened. She glances around, searching for backup. My sister does a head slide of her own. "Don't look for your friends. They've moved on to fatter, stupider targets."

Delores clenches her fists. "The cheese stands alone." She sniffs the air. "And it's stinky. Ever heard of feminine wipes? Might want to invest in some."

As hilarious and . . . disturbingly sexy . . . as this whole situation is to watch, I don't want Kate to have to deal with a wack job because of me. She's had to do that enough already. So I take the path of least resistance and grab a security guard. "We're guests at the main villa, and this . . . person"—I gesture to Psycho—"is harassing me and my fiancée. I'd like her removed from the premises immediately."

Psycho Woman doesn't take it well. "You can't do that!"

"I'm pretty sure I just did."

Security Guy checks my hotel key. "Sorry about the trouble, Mr. Evans." Then he tells her firmly, "You're going to have to come with me, miss."

"What? No—I know my rights! Don't touch me!"

When more security comes on the scene, she screeches again, like a charging boar. Before they drag her out, she spits one final threat my way. "This isn't over, asshole!"

So much for friendly skies.

Then she's gone. But the fun's not over yet. This—right here—is my favorite part.

Because Warren says, "You should've decked the bitch, Katie. I haven't seen you throw down in years."

His blonde companion may not have two brain cells to rub together, but she's loyal. "Hey—that's my friend! Bastard."

And then—

Slap.

She gets him dead in the face. Hard enough to leave an instant crimson handprint.

Blondie stomps off dramatically. While holding his flaming cheek, Warren looks at me and says, "Ugly girls don't hit so fucking hard."

Once the excitement dies down, everyone pairs off to talk and continue gambling. Leaving Kate and me relatively alone. "What was Billy saying about ugly girls?" she asks.

I wave my hand. "Irrelevant. Let's go back to the part where my dick is a compass and you're due north."

She covers her eyes. "I can't believe I said that."

I take her hands away. "Don't be embarrassed. I'm very proud. Just out of curiosity—we're talking about a monstrously huge compass, right?"

Kate pushes me on the shoulder. "Stop fishing for compliments. Let's talk about the stewardess who followed you here—am I going to have to get you a bodyguard?"

Only then do I notice her outfit. Black miniskirt, black, high-heeled boots that end just below her knee, and a sparkly pink top that leaves nothing to the imagination.

Stunning.

I walk around her like a predator circling a tasty morsel. "No, but if that's what you're wearing, I'm thinking about hiring a whole team of bodyguards for you." I finger the pink, sequined crown on her head. It says BRIDE-TO-BE. "That's a keeper."

She touches it too. "Like that, do you?"

I imagine turning it into a game. Seeing how long Kate can keep the crown balanced on her head while I do unspeakable things to her. "Very much."

"Dee-Dee got it for me."

I shrug. "Even a broken clock is right twice a day."

The broken clock herself yells, "All right, ladies—our chariot has arrived!"

Matthew cashes out our winnings. I hold Kate's hand as we all walk through the casino together. Matthew and Delores bicker playfully as we approach the lobby.

"I'm not apologizing," he tells her in a teasing voice.

"Good for you. Remember that the next time you're in the mood to play lecherous photographer and nude model—and I tell you to go screw your camera lens."

"I'm . . . I'm still not apologizing."

Do I know what they're arguing about? No. Do I care enough to ask? Not really.

We make it outside to the front entrance of the hotel. Parked at the curb is the biggest, pinkest limo I've ever freaking seen. It's like a bottle of Pepto-Bismol on wheels. Neon lights pulse on the inside, and flashing strobes spin from the roof.

I look at Dee-Dee. "A pink limo? That's not too gaudy."

She smiles proudly. "This is Vegas, baby—gaudy is king. We should retire here."

With that, she kisses Matthew and starts to walk away. Before she can take two steps, he grabs her, pulls her back, and kisses her longer and more roughly. When she's slightly dazed, Matthew grins and sends her off toward the limo. Erin waves and follows her.

I put my hands on Kate's shoulders to make sure she's paying attention. "Don't let anyone buy you a drink. And with the way you're dressed, they're definitely gonna try."

She smiles indulgently. "Okay."

"And don't put your drink down after you have it. Someone could slip something in there when you're not looking."

Yes—shit like that does happen. When you've been on the bar scene long enough, you get a clear-cut picture of just how fucked-up the world—and the people in it—are.

"Yes, Dad."

I grimace. "Don't call me that." When it comes to screwing, there's nothing I'm not into. Except that. The whole *"Who's your daddy?"* thing is a buzzkill. It's weird—it makes me think of James, or my father, and in either case . . . *no fucking thanks.*

"I'm not some twenty-one-year-old on her first trek to the bars, Drew. I can handle myself."

My sister joins the conversation. "And just in case she can't—that's what I'm here for." Alexandra pulls various weapons out of her large leather bag. "I've got my Mace, pepper spray, highly illegal Taser gun, and if all else fails . . ." She whips out a four-inch metal rod that, with a flick of her wrist, expands to the size of a police-issue nightstick—with pointy barbs on the end. "I call it the nut scrambler. Feel better now?"

I nod. "A lot better, yeah."

"Good."

She speaks quietly to Steven, then Alexandra climbs into the limo too. I wrap my arms around Kate, trying to cop one last feel. With her head on my chest, she promises, "I'll see you in a few hours."

I joke, "It's not too late to make a run for it. They'll never catch us."

She giggles. Then tilts her head up and presses her mouth softly to mine. Against my lips she murmurs, "I love you."

I pull back and trace her jaw with my fingertips. "And I will always love you more."

She smiles one final time and disappears into the bowels of the hideous limousine.

Chapter 11

After the girls' car pulls away, Matthew says, "Our ride's down thatta way, boys." He jerks his thumb toward a sleek, black stretch limo at the end of the block.

As we walk I ask Steven, "You and Alexandra get your shit straight?"

"Eh . . . not yet. But her attitude is definitely improving. I was never really worried. Your sister likes to act like she runs the show, but we all know who's really in charge."

Yeah. That would be my sister.

He pounds his chest. "I'm the man."

I don't have the heart to destroy Steven's delusions, so I just tap him on the back and say, "Yeah, Steven. You the man."

Our first stop was Carnevino, the finest steak house in Las Vegas, where we treated ourselves to a superb dinner and first-class red wine. The atmosphere was impressive—high ceilings, Italian-marble floors, antique furniture. Next we headed to Havana Club—an elite, old-school cigar bar.

That's where we are right now. See us there? In that small, private back room, sitting in cushiony leather chairs. A hand-rolled cigar in one hand and swirling an amber-liquid-filled glass in the other, while heavy-scented smoke circles our heads.

Warren lets out a choking cough for the third time.

I warn him, "Stop inhaling."

"I can't help it," he rasps. "Inhaling is like a reflex."

"You better 'help it' or you're gonna be barfing up a lung soon."

I speak from experience. When Matthew and I were twelve, we swiped a few of my father's Cubans and lit them up on the rooftop of Matthew's parents' building. Then we hurled our guts out over the edge, barely missing several unsuspecting pedestrians on the sidewalk below.

Warren sips his brandy and grimaces.

"It's an acquired taste," Steven tells him. "You'll get used to it."

Warren looks into his glass. "Why do I want to?"

"Because"—I spread my arms wide, motioning to the finely fashioned room around us—"this is the high life, man."

He wrinkles his nose. "I think I like the low life better."

I put the cigar back in my mouth and talk around it. "Again—not surprising."

Jack leans forward. "Before we move on to the main event of the night, why don't we get the toasts and roasts out of the way now?"

Steven raises his glass. "I second that motion."

I grin and stand up. "All right. I'd just like to say thank you, to you all, for taking time out of your busy schedules to share this momentous occasion with me. If I'm going out with a bang, there's nobody else I'd rather have with me than you guys." I glance at Warren. "More or less."

Then I raise my glass. "In any case, a toast: to the best friends a guy could ask for. Thank you."

We drink. There are claps and *hear, hear*s all around, then I sit down.

Warren stands up. "If we're gonna do some roasting, I should go first." The other guys give him the floor. He straightens up, clears his throat, and with a serious expression looks at each of us. "I've always thought of myself as a one-man wolf pack—"

Everyone cracks up. Who knew Warren had enough brain capacity for a sense of humor?

Matthew throws a wrapper at him. "You took my line, fucker."

Warren laughs too. "But seriously—I was a one-man wolf pack . . . with two she-wolves. And even though things were messy when Kate and Evans first hooked up, it all worked out. She's happy—and that's all I ever really wanted for her. And now, our packs have joined. And there's more wolves, and she-wolves, and wolf pups . . . the pups are cool. I guess what I'm trying to say is, I never had a big family . . . but . . . now I know what it feels like to be a part of one. It's nice."

He raises his glass in my direction. "So I'd like to toast Drew and Kate's marriage. If you ever break her heart, I'll hold you down while Dee-Dee breaks your balls."

Isn't that a lovely visual.

Still, I nod to Warren as he sits down. He takes a big chug of his drink and nods in return.

Then Jack stands. He chomps his cigar thoughtfully for a

moment. "I will never get married. I used to think Drew and I were on the same page about that. Women are like Kleenex—soft, disposable, a convenient place to cum." Everyone chuckles. "And then Kate Brooks walked into our office. And because Drew is a smart guy, he realized right away what the rest of us didn't. Kate isn't some plain, ordinary tissue. Kate is a hankie. The kind you hold on to. The kind you embroider your initials on. Kate is a keeper." Jack looks at me. "And since you're one of my best friends, I'm really glad you get to keep her for the rest of your lives." He raises his glass, "To Drew—a lucky, undeserving son of a bitch."

We raise out glasses and laughingly drink to Jack's unconventional—yet extremely accurate—toast.

Next up is Steven. He wobbles a little as he stands. He takes a big breath, holds it a moment. "Mawwiage. Mawwiage is what bwings us togethew today."

All of us laugh, except for Jack. I don't think he's seen *The Princess Bride*. It's Kate's favorite movie, so I've sat through it a few times. Definitely a chick flick—although that Inigo Montoya guy was pretty badass.

"And wuv, tru wuv, will fowow you foweva . . ." Steven grins and clears his throat. "But seriously, being the most married guy here—it's my job to warn you. Women change after marriage. It's not all candlelight dinners and lingerie, no matter what *Vogue* says. And the sex changes too. Sometimes it's routine, sometimes it's nonexistent . . . and sometimes it's freakier than you would have ever thought possible."

I cover my ears. Because usually Steven keeps his and my sister's bedroom activities to himself. And I absolutely fucking prefer it that way.

"And when you get married, the most important thing *isn't*

being in love. It's making sure you marry your best friend. A partner—the person you want to share the good times, the shitty times, and everything in between with. You've found that partner in Kate. You're my best friend, Drew—and I love you, man. But now? I get to be proud of you too. And I am—damn proud. Congratulations."

I raise my glass back at Steven. "Thanks, man. It means a lot." And it does.

Finally, Matthew takes center stage. "I am probably more grateful than anybody that Drew and Kate got together. Because of Kate, I met my angelic wife, Dee. And although sometimes she's a pain in the ass, more than anything . . . she completes me." Matthew glances down at his glass a moment, spinning the liquid around, before looking back up. "I've known Drew my whole life. We were like . . . best friends before we were born. So I've seen him have a lot of successes. I've been there when he scored the best grades, landed the biggest clients, nailed the hottest girls. And through all those times, Drew looked . . . satisfied, but unsurprised. Like all those accomplishments were just . . . expected. He worked hard for them—he always deserved them—and he knew it."

Matthew's eyes meet mine and he speaks to me directly. "But when you look at Kate? You look . . . grateful. Thankful. Like even though you know you're the shit, you still can't quite believe that you get to be the lucky bastard who has her. And . . . it's a really good look for you, man." Matthew raises his glass. "I'm not gonna wish you happiness, 'cause you've already got that. So I'll just say, may the road rise to meet you. May the wind be always at your back. May the sun shine warm upon your face. May you live as long as you want, and never want as long as you live. May there be a generation of children on the children of your children. May you live to be a hundred years, with one extra year to repent. And may the saddest day of your and Kate's future be no worse than the happiest day of your past."

By the time Matthew finishes his speech, I'm choked the fuck up. I down the rest of my drink to hide it. Then I stand up and hug him. A drunk, backslapping, lift-his-feet-off-the-floor kind of hug.

Good times . . .

After the brandy and the cigars are exhausted, we head outside. Matthew wants a cigarette; apparently the cigars didn't increase our chances of developing lung cancer enough for his liking. We hang on the corner while he lights up. Across the street is a sleek, trendy-looking bar. Loud, raucous music seeps out through the frosted, neon-framed windows, and its parking lot is filled to capacity with high-end, souped-up sports cars. Next to the bar's door, on a sidewalk bench, sits a short-haired platinum blonde with a killer body. A black tank top, denim skirt, and ankle-length, black boots show it off well. She's hot and she's alone. It's a prime opportunity for Dipshit to test out the skills I'm benevolently trying to teach him. Maybe wiggle his way under her skirt. Or possibly get Maced.

Either scenario would be a win-win in my book.

"Hey, Warren," I call. "Check it out. Lonely girl, at night, on the Vegas streets—a regular damsel in distress. Maybe you should go ask her if she needs a hand, strike up a conversation?"

Jack agrees. "The chivalry card works every time."

"Behaving like a gentleman is actually very important to me," I tell him.

"Yeah—you're a regular white knight, dude." Jack snorts.

With liquid courage flowing through his system, Warren struts across the street. He stops a few feet away from her, which is smart. Don't want to make her nervous by invading her personal space. He starts with the direct approach. "You're beautiful."

She glances up quickly, then giggles and looks away just as fast. "Thank you."

Warren inches closer. "So . . . you need a ride? We're not serial killers or anything. Just a few guys, hanging out. And we have a limo. You could hang with us or I could give you a lift, wherever you wanted to go."

Her head turns toward the bar, just a bit nervously. "I'm supposed to wait here for my boyfriend."

Warren sits beside her on the bench. "I don't know what kind of man leaves a gorgeous woman like you sitting out on the street. If you were my girl, I'd never do that."

Good boy. I feel that I should throw him a treat or pat his head.

And then . . .

"What the fuck did you just say?"

That little tidbit was growled by a beefy, blond-haired guy who just walked out from the side of the bar, with four other equally large men behind him. What they lack in height, they make up for in solid girth—the type my mother would have called "big boned." They're probably early to mid-twenties; one has a University of Nevada hat on, another wears a sweatshirt with Greek lettering.

Frat boys.

Although I was one of them once, I never realized how fucking obnoxious and annoying this particular breed can be, until after I graduated. They epitomize the phrase *young, dumb, and full of cum*. Because they travel in groups, they have that mob mentality—emboldened, loud, and constantly trying to impress each other how far up the dick-o-meter their actions are.

And Billy Warren is in their crosshairs. Not good.

Warren begins to respond, "I said—"

I jog over, with Jack, Matthew, and Steven hot on my heels, to make sure Warren doesn't get killed. Kate would not be pleased.

Blond Ape #1 shoves Warren's chest. The really strange thing is, it genuinely pisses me off. "You talkin' to my girlfriend, loser?" He grabs the girl by the arm. "I told you to wait, bitch—I didn't say you could talk."

I step in front of Billy. "Hey, fellas—I think there's been a little misunderstanding."

"I don't think this is any of your business."

I confess, "You have no idea how much I wish that were true. Unfortunately, it's not. My friend thought the girl needed help. He was looking out for her—that's all. No harm, no foul."

"Your boyfriend made a major fucking foul, hitting on my girl. I'm gonna take it out on his ass." Then he spits at my feet.

Classy.

I no longer feel like resolving this diplomatically. "Well, if you're gonna be an asshole about it—"

The girl tries to intervene. She puts a hand on the guy's chest while the other rubs his arm, trying to soothe the savage beast. "He didn't do anything. Just let it go, Blair."

I can't help but chuckle. "*Blair?* Your name is Blair? Christ, no wonder you're so angry. You have my sincerest sympathy." Keeping my eyes on the group of numb-nuts, I motion to Matthew. "You see what happens when parents are careless with the naming? This is your future, man."

In case you can't tell—no, I'm not intimidated by the loudmouth frat boy. Because he, like most bullies, is a pussy. Real tough guys? Truly dangerous men? They're on the quiet side. They don't need to put on a show or announce all the pain they're going to inflict on you. They just do it, before you ever have the chance to be afraid. Or see it coming.

Blair steps toward me, but Warren pops in between us—hands raised in submission.

"Hold up. Just wait—this is between you and me, fucker. Keep my friends out of it."

I look at Warren as if he's lost his mind. 'Cause I'm fairly certain that's the case. "Are you nuts?"

He looks back over his shoulder at me. "Katie would never forgive me if you missed the wedding because you were in the hospital. And I grew up with Dee-Dee—if there's one thing I know how to do, it's take a beating."

Right then and there, my opinion of Warren is forever altered. He's still an idiot—as he just demonstrated. And because of his history with Kate, I'll never like him. But throwing himself on his sword like this? Trying to protect me and the guys? It takes balls—brass ones. He just earned my respect.

Matthew, Steven, and Jack are lined up behind me, tense and ready. I take a breath and ask, "Matthew—you cool with this plan?"

He answers, "Absolutely."

"How about you, Jack, you up for it?"

He chuckles darkly. "I'm always up for it, man."

"Steven?"

"Why the hell not? Screw it."

Those are the only answers I need. I step around Warren, closer to Blair. "Okay—you can kick the shit out of him, and the rest of us will just sit by and watch."

Confused shock registers on his face. "Seriously?"

I smile. "No, moron—I'm lying to you." By the time my words register in his addled brain, my fist is already flying. Right at the fucker's nose, busting it wide-open.

Then all hell breaks loose.

Typically, I believe a sucker punch is a pansy move. Cowardly. But this is a street fight. A cage match. There are no rules. Fingers in the eye sockets, kicks to the nads—it's all fair game. A bloodied Blair tackles me to the ground, while the melee rages around us.

I take a blow to the shoulder and the ribs, trying to protect my face. Warren had a valid point about the wedding thing. If my face is stitched up like Frankenstein's, it'll ruin the pictures.

I land a left hook to the dickhead's jaw, close enough to the injured nose to make him howl. It goes on like this for about five minutes, though it feels much longer.

Then the girl that started it all says the magic words: "Cops! Cops!"

Every one of us responds like a high schooler at a beer bash.

We run. We break apart and scatter. The five of us make it back to the confines of the limo in record time, and the driver takes off. The flashing lights of Las Vegas's finest don't follow us. Thank God.

You may not understand it, but believe me when I tell you this was an awesome development to our evening. No matter how old he is, every guy thinks it's cool to drink, gamble, and then beat the shit out of somebody with his closest friends. We pass around a bottle of vodka and show off our battle wounds, bragging about how great we were.

"Did you see that guy's teeth explode? Bam!"

"I had that big son of a bitch on the ropes. He was ready to cry for his ugly mama."

"Hope that loser likes liquid meals, 'cause that's all he's gonna be able to have for a long time."

I take a sip of Grey Goose, then pour it on my bleeding knuckles.

Warren shakes his head and laments, "My luck with girls is crap."

No one disagrees. But what I've come to accept is this: it's not his fault.

Really.

Warren is simply more pussy than dick. It's how he was raised—surrounded by bush. It's like . . . one of those weird news stories about a baby tiger that's adopted by a family of pigs. When it's older, it doesn't show its claws or pounce or growl.

It fucking oinks.

Unlike the rest of us, who had confident, strong men in our lives, Warren's only male exposure was whatever specimens Amelia brought home. Obviously, there were no freaking winners in that bunch.

After a minute, he asks, "I really thought you were gonna let them kick my ass. What changed?"

Matthew takes a drink from the bottle. "Fuck that. No man gets left behind."

I nod. "Exactly. You know the first rule of wolf packs?"

"What?"

"We take care of our own."

Chapter 12

I think we should step back and take note of just how much alcohol the boys and I have consumed so far. There were the shots and beers at the pool, the Scotches in the room and at the casino, the wine with dinner, the brandy afterward, and now the vodka that we're passing around like winos huddled near a burning garbage can.

I'm no lightweight—but that's a lot of fucking booze. We're out-and-out walking saloons, for God's sake. Even though it's been spread out over hours, eventually that shit catches up to you. One minute you've got it all under control, then you take that last shot. The scales get tipped, and you find yourself on the floor—unable to walk or form a coherent sentence without drooling.

Remember this fact.

I have a feeling it's going to play a big part in whatever lies ahead.

Looking out the window at the dark desert landscape, I ask, "Where are we going again?"

Matthew and Jack grin at each other. Jack says, "We're going to heaven, brother. No lie—this place is like an oasis. Top-of-the-line women who know how to take care of a man. Nothing is off-limits—T and A will be everywhere." He kisses his fingers. "Like manna from heaven."

I just shrug, unimpressed. But apparently Warren's impatient. "Driver dude? What's the holdup? I can get out and walk faster than this."

The driver glances back at us in the rearview mirror. "Sorry, fellas. There's a Lincoln Town Car in front of me doin' twenty below the speed limit. She won't let me pass her."

I sit up and glance out the front window. Yep—it's a grayhair. A whole clown car full of grayhairs, actually. You remember my feelings about senior-citizen drivers? In case you don't, I'll just say this: menace to society.

Steven holds the bottle of vodka and takes a swig. I don't know if he's talking to us or himself, but out of nowhere he says, "I'm going to be dead soon."

All eyes in the limo turn to him. Matthew asks, "What the hell are you talking about?"

"I'm talking about my life is half over. And there's so much I haven't done. I'm not going to hold back anymore—I'm going carpe diem on this bitch from here on out."

I scoff. "You're just trashed. Don't go getting depressed on us now. If you start crying, I'm throwing you out of the car while it's still moving."

Steven doesn't acknowledge my warning. He leans toward the partition separating us from the driver and slurs, "I'll give you a hundred bucks if you can get up alongside 'em."

With no oncoming traffic, the driver crosses the double line and pulls even with the Lincoln.

Steven's words slush together as he gets to his feet. "Crossing this one off the bucket list." Then he unbuckles his belt and grabs the waist of his pants—yanking the suckers down to his ankles—tighty whities and all.

Every guy in the car holds up his hands to try to block the spectacle. We groan and complain. "My eyes! They burn!"

"Put the boa constrictor back in his cage, man."

"This is not the ass I planned on seeing tonight."

Our protests fall on deaf ears. Steven is a man on a mission. Wordlessly, he squats and shoves his lily-white ass out the window—mooning the gaggle of grannies in the car next to us.

I bet you thought this kind of stuff only happened in movies.

He grins while his ass blows in the wind for a good ninety seconds, ensuring optimal viewage. Then he pulls his slacks up, turns around, and leans out the window, laughing. "Enjoying the full moon, ladies?"

Wow. Steven usually isn't the type to visually assault the elderly.

Without warning, his crazy cackling is cut off. He's silent for a beat, then I hear him choke out a single strangled word.

"Grandma?"

Then he's diving back into the limo, his face grayish, dazed, and totally sober. He stares at the floor. "No way that just happened."

Matthew and I look at each other hopefully, then we scramble to the window. Sure enough, in the driver's seat of that big old Town Car is none other than Loretta P. Reinhart. Mom to George; Grandma to Steven.

What are the fucking odds, huh?

Loretta was always a cranky old bitch. No sense of humor. Even when I was a kid she hated me. Thought I was a bad influence on her precious grandchild.

Don't know where she got that idea from.

She moved out to Arizona years ago. Like a lot of women her age, she still enjoys a good tug on the slot machine—hence her frequent trips to Sin City. Apparently this is one such trip.

Matthew and I wave and smile and in fourth-grader-like, singsong harmony call out, "Hi, Mrs. Reinhart."

She shakes one wrinkled fist in our direction. Then her poofy-haired companion in the backseat flips us the bird. I'm pretty sure it's the funniest goddamn thing I've ever seen.

The two of us collapse back into our seats, laughing hysterically.

Steven snaps out of his stupor and yells to the driver, "For the love of God, man, floor it!"

We speed off into the night, howling like Mad Hatters on laughing gas. All of us except Steven. You know that saying "What happens in Vegas stays in Vegas"? I don't think my brother-in-law is gonna be that lucky.

The name of the strip club is Paradise. The sand-colored, two-story, windowless building is surrounded with lush trees, stone statues, a pond, and several fountains. The oasislike atmosphere stands out in sharp contrast to the barren desert around it. Even though the sign glows a modern neon, I half expect to see girls in togas, carrying big palm leaves and frigging grapes, wandering around the outside.

We get to the front door. You may want to brace yourself. Don't want anyone keeling over from the shock. Because, you have to understand—men are essentially pigs in human clothing. I readily admit it. There is no end to the perverted high jinks, fetishes, fortes, and fantasies we're capable of dreaming up.

And this joint caters to every single one of them.

The door is opened by a fortyish-looking redhead in a dark green teddy with matching heels. She has aristocratic features—pale skin, full lips, high cheekbones—nicely accentuated by expensively subtle plastic surgery. "Welcome to Paradise, gentlemen. We've been expecting you."

Cream-colored walls, marble tile, and a burning white-stone fireplace make the foyer feel welcoming and warm. Almost homey. Deep, sexy music pounds from behind a dark mahogany door on the far side of the room. "My name is Carla; I'll be your hostess this evening. If there is anything I can get for you during your stay—anything at all—please don't hesitate to ask."

Warren's mouth hangs open—like a fish who's seen the face of God. Matthew and Jack are giggly with anticipation, while Steven still looks dazed from mooning his grandma.

But I bet he'll forget all about that shortly. We walk into the next room. The lights are low—as they always are in places like this—but the room is huge for a strip club. A main stage sits in the center, with two smaller stages beside it, each with a standard silver pole. A large glass bar lines one wall, with two bikini-clad dancers swaying on top.

Men of all ages are scattered everywhere—at small tables, corner booths, and bar stools. And every one of them has at least two girls fawning over him. Out of the corner of my eye I see a salt-and-pepper-haired guy motorboating the tits of a blonde with pigtails and a Catholic-schoolgirl uniform. Behind them, a black-haired Asian woman stands naked on a table, sliding a Blow Pop into her twat. Then she leans down and pops it into the mouth of the college-age kid salivating in front of her.

Kind of reminds you of Sodom or Gomorrah, doesn't it? And we all know how they ended up.

I tried to warn you.

Carla explains, "To the left is our game room. I've reserved a poker table for your party as you requested, Matthew. Darts and billiards are also available. Down that hall are the booths for private dances, and upstairs we have fully appointed rooms for even more private interactions, should you desire."

She leads us to the bar. "First round is on the house. This is Jane." Carla motions to a dark-haired girl behind the bar, wearing a suit jacket and nothing else. "She'll be your private server."

Warren's eyes follow a long-legged blonde wearing assless leather chaps as she walks by. "I thought it was against the law to have naked girls and alcohol in the same place."

Matthew shakes his head. "That's only in New York and Jersey. This is the land of legalized prostitution."

I hold up a finger. "But all other rules apply. Which means no touching, unless somebody tells you otherwise."

Warren's mouth is still hanging open. I close it ungently. "Get a grip, man. Don't embarrass us or I'll make you go sit in the car."

He forces his face to relax. Then he bobs his head and slumps his shoulders. "No, it's good. I'm cool. I'm . . . holy shit! Do you see that chick with the lollipop?!"

Hopeless.

I turn away. "Jane, I'll take a whiskey on the rocks, please."

Service with a smile. "Coming right up, Mr. Evans."

Carla takes her leave. "I'll be close by should you need my assistance. Enjoy your evening, gentlemen." As soon as she steps away, five girls converge on us, each more stunning than the next.

I sip my whiskey as one blue-lingerie-clad stripper meets my eyes. "So this is a bachelor party? And you're the groom?"

I smile. "That's me."

"I love grooms."

Small talk with strippers is not really the norm. Usually it's more of a transaction: rubbing and gyrating in exchange for a few singles. But this isn't your typical strip club. And I'm a friendly guy. "How come?"

"They're always the wildest ones."

"Not me. Tonight is more for my buddies. I'm just an innocent bystander."

She giggles and pinches my cheek. "You don't look innocent." She gives my face a mini slap. "You look more like the naughty type."

I wink. "Guilty as charged."

A curly-haired girl with wide hips, wearing a purple bikini and standing next to Jack, vies for my attention next. "You wanna see a magic trick?"

"Sure."

Out of nowhere, she holds up a large cucumber. "I'm going to make this cucumber disappear. Watch closely." She peels off her bikini bottoms, spreads her legs, and inserts the end of the cucumber into her pussy. Then she holds her hands up over her head. Her abdominal muscles clench, and magically the cucumber slides up, disappearing into her twat.

Now all of our mouths are hanging open like Warren's.

Then, the cucumber peeks out and slides down. She grabs it and says sweetly, "Ta-da!"

I clap my hands. "You are a very talented girl."

Yes—I'm going to hell. But at least I'll be in good company.

Jack holds up his hands, fingers spread. "I give it a ten for creativity."

Matthew adds, "You'd be a shoo-in for that *X Factor* show."

She just smirks at me. "How about a private dance and I can show you all of my talents?"

I shrug her off. "Maybe later."

One hour, a few drinks, and about a hundred $1 bills later, Carla rejoins our little group. "I hope you gentlemen are enjoying yourselves?"

While I pass the time watching two girls tongue-kissing each other at the direction of a middle-aged patron, Matthew answers, "We are, thank you. The service and amenities are impeccable."

"We aim to please. And now it's time to give the guest of honor a true Paradise welcome." She takes my arm. "If you'll come with me, Drew?"

That takes my attention away from the Female Foreplay Show. "I'm fine right here, thanks."

She smiles persuasively. "I'm afraid it's not optional. Your friends insisted."

I frown at the guys. "What did you douche bags do?"

Matthew laughs sinisterly. "Nothing you weren't expecting."

"It's your last night of freedom, man. Enjoy it," Jack adds.

Two more girls come up behind me. They and Carla pull me off my stool and guide me onstage as Steven yells out, "It'll only hurt for a minute!"

I decide to go with the flow. It was too much to hope that the guys didn't have some sick, twisted event planned. Best to just get it over with now. A lone chair sits empty in the middle of the stage. As three pairs of feminine hands push me down in it, the lights dim even lower. Spotlights dance around the room, and when "One More Night" by Maroon 5 comes on, the crowd cheers.

Two woman bounce out from backstage. They're wearing black G-strings and sheer, black button-down tops. After a few ass shakes and high kicks for the crowd, they turn toward me. One drops to her knees and crawls around my legs like a submissive—and appealing—kitten.

Her hands slide up my calves to my knees and she pushes—roughly jerking them apart. Then she ties each ankle to the leg of the chair with a surprisingly sturdy ribbon. The girl in back scratches red fingernails down my chest, stopping just above the danger zone. Then she yanks both my arms back and ties my wrists behind me. It's not exactly enjoyable. Some guys like to be dominated, but as history has shown, I'm much more of the dominator type.

But my interest is piqued. The crowd goes wild as another woman appears front and center—swinging gracefully around the pole, obviously the star of the show. She's petite, but thigh-high, leather, black boots with insanely spiked heels make her seem taller. Her hair is tucked under a black leather cap, shocking red gloss covers her lips, and dark sunglasses disguise much of her face. The rest of her body, however, is bared for all to see. A black thong with a scarcely there triangle hangs on her hips. Her tits are adorned with stick-on nipple tassels—and nothing else.

With her back to me, she rips off the cap and throws it to the crowd, revealing a cascade of shiny, brown hair. She takes a few more spins on the pole, then turns toward me and stalks forward.

For a moment, I'd swear on my kid that it was Kate. The face and body dimensions are *that* similar.

Upon closer inspection, I notice the differences, however. Besides the fact that Kate Brooks would never be up on a stage shaking her tits and ass in the faces of strangers—unless she actually *wanted* me to stick ice picks through the eyeballs of every asshole in the place.

And, yes, that would include the assholes I came with.

But also, this girl's skin is paler than my fiancée's, her nose thinner, her hair lighter—not quite the same mahogany shade. Other than that, the resemblance is pretty fucking frightening.

She spins and leans against me, her back pressed up against my chest. Her hair falls across my face and tickles my nose. She smells . . . great. Like honeysuckle and jasmine. It's a musky incense, like the aroma of a closed room after hours of fantastic fucking. She doesn't smell nearly as incredible as Kate—but her bouquet is what I would've probably defined as incredible if I'd never had the pleasure of Kate's sublime scent.

Her arms snake around my neck and her ass nestles perfectly against my dick. Then she slides down between my open legs and arches forward elegantly, raising her ass tantalizingly toward my face. She plants her feet on the floor and straightens her legs, while still bent over at the waist. Then she slides the thong down her legs and smacks her right butt cheek hard—in the way I'm sure every guy in the place is chomping at the bit to do.

She stands up and turns to face me again. She kicks one leg slowly up around my head—giving me an unobstructed, detailed display of her bare slit.

I swear I try not to look. Really.

But I do.

Give me a motherfucking break—I'm engaged, not dead.

She climbs onto my lap, facing me. Then she shoves the thong she'd been wearing in my mouth. The crowd roars to a deafening crescendo.

I think the crazy train just jumped the track. I'd like to get off now—and not in the happy way. It's all fun and games until you have another woman's bodily fluids on your tongue. Kate would never be okay with this. Remind me to guzzle some Listerine when we get back to the room.

Her red lips smile as she snatches the tie off my neck, and I manage to spit out the thong. Unperturbed, she drapes the open tie around my shoulders and holds each side like a horse's reins. She wraps the ends around her hands and uses them for leverage. Her hips sway and swivel expertly, the way only an experienced dancer—or expensive hooker—knows how.

To my utter horror—my cock gets hard. He moves quickly into position—rigid and ready.

Since the day Kate let me fuck her, I, and my dick, haven't given any other women a second glance. No matter how attractive or available, we haven't been interested. Or aroused.

Not one frigging time.

It feels completely wrong. To use Kate's words—it's like a

compass pointing south. If that were to happen, it would mean the universe was off-kilter. The end of the world as we know it. That's almost what this seems like.

Like a betrayal.

Maybe the priests were right, after all. Maybe penises are evil.

I glare down at my lap.

Traitor.

Chapter 13

After the stage lights go dark and I'm untied from the chair, I can't get off the stage quickly enough. I make a beeline for my happy place, also known as the bar.

The guys surround me, backslapping and laughing like chimpanzees at the zoo. "That was awesome!"

"I'm rethinking this whole marriage thing. If it gets me a fucking show like that, I just might do it."

"I'll take those seconds any day. . . . Wasn't anything sloppy about that brunette!"

A thousand frazzled thoughts race through my head at once, but I put up a solid front.

"It was great." Talk quickly turns to joining the poker game in the back room. As the others make their way over, Matthew turns back to me, where I'm still sitting at the bar.

"You okay, man?"

I lick my dry lips. "Yeah, I'm good. Just going to finish my drink."

He nods understandingly and leaves me on my own. Have to admit, I'm a little bit shaky. What was that hard-on all about? Did it happen because the woman grinding on me looked so much like Kate? And most important, do I have to tell Kate about it?

Jesus.

I go from looking at my drink to swallowing it in .5 seconds. There's no way I'm telling Kate.

Don't look at me like that. Whoever said honesty was the best policy never lived with a frigging chick. Sometimes, it's best to keep your mouth shut. Certain things women don't want to know—things, like this, that will accomplish nothing but upsetting them.

I'm comfortable with my decision . . . until someone taps me on the shoulder.

I turn around to find a pair of big, beautiful brown eyes smiling at me. If my cock had an elbow, he'd nudge me with it.

She's changed since the stage show. Or, should I say, covered up. She's wearing a red, lace, knee-length nightie, with matching high heels. It's actually pretty conservative for a place like this. Close up, I note that her skin is creamy white and clear—with almost no makeup. Her hair is still down, straight and shiny, and soft looking.

She greets me with a cheery "Hi."

"Hey."

"I'm Lily."

I nod.

"Are you having fun tonight?"

I motion to the bartender for another. "Sure, it's . . . super."

Lily sits—uninvited—on the stool next to mine. "I'm glad. I wanted to make sure you enjoyed the show, because I'm new here. I only started a few weeks ago."

The revelation surprises me. "Never would've guessed. You're a natural."

Her smile gets wider. "Wow, you're so sweet." Her voice drops to a whisper, as if she were about to spill top-secret information. "But I'm not really a stripper, you know."

I look around the room. Then I look her up and down. "Is it some elaborate game of make-believe?"

She laughs. "I'm a student, actually. This is my last year at the University of Nevada."

I remark drily, "A student stripping her way through college? How very stereotypical of you."

She rolls her eyes. Not unlike the way Kate does frequently. "I waitressed at Hooters for a year. But with the economy the way it is, they had cutbacks. And I got let go last month."

"I always thought tits and ass were recession-proof."

She shrugs and sips her drink. "Didn't we all."

I toy with the napkin on the bar, feeling Lily's eyes appraising me. "What?"

"You just . . . you're nothing like the other grooms I've seen in this place. They acted like I was their last meal before the execution. But you're different. It's nice."

Although she seems sincere, I'm suspicious of the nice-girl-just-trying-to-get-by act. Strippers get naked for money—that's the job. They get more money if the customers like them—if the stripper can make them feel they're special. Different. "I don't do this for just any guy," they say, and—bam—before the loser knows it, his whole paycheck is down the drain.

Or up the crotch, in this case.

Lily puts her hand on my leg, and she starts to rub—moving higher and higher. "How about we go in the back for a private dance? I'll even do you for free. It'll be my pleasure."

What'd I tell you? Can I call them, or can I call them?

I stop her wandering hand with my own. "I can't."

She leans toward me and tries again. "Sure you can."

But I hold my ground. "I could. But I won't."

She stops, finally getting the point. Looking a little confused, she asks, "Do you have one of those crazy, controlling fiancées? The kind that makes you promise no lap dances, even at your bachelor party?"

I shake my head. "Not at all. I don't think she'd be pissed. But . . . I think she'd be hurt."

That's what no one tells you about being in love. Sure it's grand and amazing and feels fucking fantastic. But there's stress too. Obligation. Responsibility. The knowledge that someone else's happiness—someone who means so much to you—can be made or destroyed by the choices you make. By the things you do.

Or in my case, the things you don't.

"I've done that before—made a bad call. Hurt her. And I'm determined not to ever do it again."

Lily's eyes glaze over with admiration. She's probably not used to talking to a guy who isn't a complete and utter dickweed. For her, it must be like when those scientists in the sixties first realized apes were capable of learning sign language. A revelation.

She kisses her fingertip and presses it to my cheek. "I hope your fiancée knows how lucky she is, Drew."

I smirk. "I make sure to remind her every day."

She smiles longingly. Then her gaze turns to the other end of the room, where an expensive-suit-wearing older gentleman sits by himself, looking all kinds of lonely.

She hops off the bar chair. "Duty calls." In a flurry of dark hair, she walks away.

My eyes follow her as she goes. And, *thank Christ*, my dick doesn't move an inch.

Before she reaches her destination, I get an idea. Practice makes perfect—and there's no better practice run than a newly minted stripper.

I call her back. "I'm gonna pay for that private dance after all."

Her eyes light up. "Okay."

"But it's not for me."

I guide her to the back room, where Warren is playing poker—badly—with Steven, Jack, and Matthew. "Hey, douche bag, have you ever had a private dance?"

Suspicion washes over his face, probably thinking I'm setting him up to be the butt of a joke. Not that he needs any help in that department. "No, I haven't. Why?"

I smile and motion to each of them with my hand. "Lily, this is Billy. Billy—Lily."

Warren stands and Lily loops her arm around his. "First timer, huh? I'll take good care of you."

I'm just racking up the good deeds today, aren't I? I tap both their shoulders. "You kids have fun."

As they walk away together, I hear Warren ask, "Have you heard the one about the priest and the rabbi in a bar?"

I close my eyes and shake my head. *Fucking hopeless.*

I tell the poker dealer to deal me in, then lay my money on the table and stack the green chips she slides my way. Without prompting, a shot girl places a fresh whiskey in front of me, and I put my tip on the tray. Paradise isn't your run-of-the-mill strip club. It's not just about the dancers—it's about making the customers feel like kings. Anticipating their wants and desires.

Jack changes two cards and comments, "Drew Evans turning down a lap dance—that makes me sad."

"I turned it down out of respect for Kate. Just like she canceled the man massage out of respect for me."

Steven smiles and congratulates me. "You've come so far, Little Grasshopper."

I grin. "Kate and I have a very respectful relationship."

This is mostly true. Although, at times a little disrespect can end up being a really good time.

Let's examine that theory more closely:

After what feels like an eternity of not being inside Kate, our six-week sex ban has at last come to an end. My generous parents—whom I love tonight more than ever—agreed to come to our apartment and watch James for a few hours.

My cock has fabulous, filthy ideas on how to spend every minute of those hours.

Despite his intentions, we didn't go straight to the hotel room I rented for the evening. Why not? you ask. The short answer is because Kate owns me, I'm now a pushover—and a fucking idiot. The long answer is because Kate put extra effort into getting dressed for our night together—she painted her toenails, curled her hair just so, and bought a scorching-hot little black dress that makes her tits look fantastic. Meaning she wants to spend at least part of the night in public. Around other adults.

Engaging in conversation that will stimulate her mind as acutely as I plan on stimulating her clit with my tongue very shortly.

So . . . we're eating dinner at Jean-Georges, an ultrachic restau-

rant that also happens to be located one block from our hotel suite. Talk during dinner was interesting and fun, as always. We talked about James, work, Kate's upcoming transition back to the office, and my impending conversion to part-time stay-at-home dad. The food was great too. Yet it hasn't exactly been an enjoyable meal for me.

My body is strung tight with anticipation, and every single thing Kate does just makes me want to fuck her that much more. The way her fingers grasp her water glass, the way she licks her lips and slides the fork deep into her mouth.

Christ.

It's a blessing you can't actually die from horniness—'cause I'd be stone cold by now.

Even though Kate's been strict about what she eats, because she's breast-feeding and working hard to get back into her "skinny" jeans, I talked her into indulging in some dessert.

Not my best idea.

"Mmmm . . . ," she moans over a bite of chocolate cake.

My dick twitches—like a wild bull raring to get out of his pen.

I swallow the rest of my wine, reminding myself it'll only be a few more minutes until I have her all to myself. Naked. With no one and nothing to disturb us for four blissful hours.

Kate pushes her plate back and wipes her mouth elegantly with her napkin. Then she regards me thoughtfully. "I've been wondering about something."

"What are you wondering?" I'm surprised that my voice is actually level. Considering the crotch of my pants is now painfully snug.

"Do you remember the night we met—at REM?"

I lean forward in my chair and run my finger up and down her bare arm. "Every provocative detail."

She likes my answer. She smiles. "What do you think would've happened if I had gone home with you that night?"

I force my gaze up from Kate's impressive rack to meet her eyes. "I would've done exactly what I said—given the word pleasure *a whole new meaning."*

"But what about afterward?"

This is one of those tricky hypothetical questions women love to pose—just to screw with a guy's head. "What if you had met my sister first?" "Would you have respected me if I fucked you on the first date?" "If you could go back in time, would you still marry me?"

Contrary to popular belief, there's definitely a right way and a wrong way to answer. Unfortunately for men, the honest answer is usually the wrong one.

But because I've sworn to never lie to Kate again—and because she'll know if I am *frigging lying—I go with the truth.*

"Afterward, I would've paid your cab fare and gone on my own merry, sexually satisfied way home." I wink. "And I would've ranked our night as the best of my life. So far."

She doesn't frown, exactly, but the potential is there. Disappointment settles in her brown eyes, and the edges of her smile fall just a bit.

"That's it? So you don't think we'd be together right now?"

I pick up her hand and hold it in mine, looking it over before kissing each of her fingertips. "I didn't say that. Like those of most geniuses, my epiphanies take a little time to settle in. I would've spent most of Sunday reminiscing—but by Sunday night, I would've started figuring out how to find you again."

Just like that, the pre-frown vanishes. "You would've wanted seconds?"

"Seconds, thirds, fourths . . . and when I found you at my office on Monday? You can bet your ass my couch would've been scandalized much sooner."

Kate leans forward, purposely teasing me with a bird's-eye view of her cleavage. "What about your rule—Drew Evans doesn't ride the same roller coaster twice?"

I enjoy the scenery.

"I've proven beyond a reasonable doubt that when it comes to you, my rules were always meant to be broken. If you were the coaster in question, I would've bought the whole fucking amusement park and ridden you until I couldn't see straight."

Kate's free hand slides up my thigh, inching close to the holy land. Her voice is teasing. Playful. "Are you flirting with me, Mr. Evans?"

"If you have to ask, I'm obviously out of practice." I up my game. "Take your panties off. Right here, right now. Then give them to me."

How's that for flirting?

Her hand stops its exploration. "I'm afraid I can't do that."

She doesn't sound shy or shocked. So I know her refusal isn't because she doesn't want to.

The lewd lightbulb goes on above my head. "You're not wearing any, are you?"

Kate looks into my eyes. And sexily pops the p *as she says, "Nope."*

Instantly my finger rises toward the waiter. "Check, please."

The waiter quickly brings the check, and I throw a handful of bills down on the table. In a rush, I stand up.

Kate giggles. "They're going to think you're unhappy about the food, Drew."

I help her out of her seat and lower my mouth to her ear. "I don't give a shit what they think. If I don't get you out of here right now, I'm going to lay you down on this table and give the other customers a show they'll never forget."

She looks up at my face daringly. "And I'd let you."

Oblivious of the stares of the patrons and staff, Kate wraps her arms around my neck and kisses me. When her demanding tongue strokes mine, the sensation goes straight to my balls. With my arm around her lower back, I say, "You got all dolled up—I thought you wanted a night out."

"Drew, I haven't come in six weeks. The only thing I want is your cock so deep inside me, I can taste it."

I don't actually remember leaving the restaurant after that. Kate's awesomely dirty revelation must have fried my brain.

The next thing I know, we're on the sidewalk and I'm dragging her to the side of the building—to the narrow alley just wide enough to fit a Dumpster that faces the street. I have enough awareness to bring Kate to the far side of it—so we're shielded from the view of cars and pedestrians. My eyes scan the path for intruders. Finding none, I devote all of my attention to Kate—to making up for all the screwless days she's endured.

My hand buries itself in her hair, gripping the soft strands, holding her head captive as I plunder her mouth with my tongue. She writhes and rubs against me, pulling my shirt free of my pants and working on my belt.

It's times like this I wish God had made people more like octopuses—six extra hands would be convenient right about now. We're ravenous for each other—tearing and pulling at annoying clothes, wanting to touch every erogenous zone at the same time.

It reminds me of the first time we kissed, that night in my office years ago. It feels the same as that night—I'd wanted Kate, fantasized about her for weeks then too. The difference now is, I know precisely what I've been fucking missing. So I'm even hungrier for her, bordering on totally out of control.

My hand slides down the front of her dress, into her bra, straining the fabric. I palm and knead her full breast, and a welcome moan reverberates in Kate's throat. My fingers rub and pinch her nipple, making it harden to a perfect peak. Kate tears her mouth from mine and moves to my neck—sucking and licking—nipping the sensitive skin with her teeth. Making me weak in the fucking knees.

I switch gears and slide my hands up her thighs, bunching her dress above her waist. Then I kneel down and pause for just a moment to appreciate the sight of her exquisitely smooth snatch.

Panting hard, Kate tries to cover her stomach with her hands. "I know I'm not—"

"Don't fucking finish that sentence." I grab her wrists, holding them away from her body.

Pregnancy is a strange experience for women. So many fast-paced changes—mentally, emotionally, physically. And, no, Kate doesn't look exactly as she did before. But only a total asshole would expect her to.

Only the eminent ruler of all assholes would care.

"You made a person, Kate. A perfectly amazing person." Then I look up into her eyes and tell her honestly, "You've never been more beautiful to me than you are right now."

A smile tugs at her flushed lips. I release her wrists, lean forward, and press my mouth against the soft flesh of her pussy.

Hello, old friend. I've missed you.

I spread her with my fingers and delve in deep. She's hot on my tongue—already wet—and sweeter than chocolate frigging cake. I cup her ass in my hands, pressing her forward, and revel in the taste of her. My eyes roll back in my head as Kate moans and gasps above me. Her fingernails cut into my shoulder blades, and after only a minute she's begging.

"Please, Drew . . . I need you inside me. I need to feel you now."

Unwilling to deny her and incapable of it, I lap at her one last time and stand. I cover her lips with mine and back us up to the wall of the building. As I caress her tits, Kate slips my pants and boxers down my hips.

She takes my straining cock in her hands, pumping it firmly and slowly.

I groan into her mouth.

Then I lift her, cushioning the back of her head with one hand, so it doesn't smack against the bricks. My other arm is under her ass, holding her up. Kate locks her ankles together at my lower back, then guides my dick home.

I don't wait. Waiting is just not possible. I plunge into her roughly, deeply.

"Drew . . . ," she sighs.

Kate's wet inner walls stretch around me, still blissfully fucking snug. Buried fully, I savor the sensation of being inside her again. Being surrounded and held by intense, hot perfection.

I whisper the only word that matters. "Kate . . ."

Her legs pull me closer, knees squeezing tighter. I do what we're both craving.

I move.

Slowly, my hips pull back. Kate's cunt grips my cock spectacularly as it slides from her.

"You feel like fucking heaven," I moan.

Then I thrust forward hard, rubbing her clit with my pelvis, making sure she's feeling the same blinding pleasure I am. I keep that pace—slow, rough strokes that make Kate purr every time our bodies collide.

Her eyes close and her mouth finds mine.

We're gasping and moaning, gripping and pulsing—drowning in fantastic friction. With her cheek pressed against mine, Kate pants, "Oh, God . . . oh, God, Drew, I'm going to come."

My hips quicken, needing to feel her contracting around me more than I need air to breathe. "Fuck yes, come, baby. Let me feel you come hard."

Then she is. Her arms around my neck, her legs around my waist, constrict and tighten. Kate's pussy squeezes my cock in a primal, uncontrollable rhythm that pulls me deeper inside her. I push and surge forward one last time, until I rise into the stratosphere with her. It's so fucking good, so intense, for several long, exquisite moments the only sound I can hear is the rush of our ecstasy pounding in my ears.

Minutes later, I'm still breathing deep against Kate's neck, and she continues to tremble with aftershocks. Still inside her, I lift my head and brush her hair from her face.

"That was awesome."

She smiles wide. "Mind-blowing."

Carefully, I set her feet back on solid ground. Then I help smooth her dress back into place and tuck myself in and zip up. "And we still have a whole suite waiting for us."

"Take me to my suite." Kate holds out her hand.

I take it. "It'll be my pleasure."

Literally.

Back out on the sidewalk, the fog of lust clears and Kate puts the hand I'm not holding over her eyes. "I can't believe we had sex in an alley."

I snort. "I can't believe we waited so long to have sex in an alley. What was I thinking?"

That's an activity that's definitely going on my repeat list.

Is alley-screwing respectful? Generally . . . no. But in this case, it was just what the doctor ordered.

Now, back to our card game.

Jack turns to Steven. "What do you say, Reinhart—you and me and two of the most flexible ladies in the club?"

"Alexandra would rip my head off if I got a lap dance—private or otherwise," Steven laments.

Matthew grins. "Delores would be into it—but only if she got to watch."

Steven shakes his head. "I don't want to give her another reason to be pissed at me."

Matthew chuckles. "But that's the way it works, man. Dee-Dee's happier when I'm messing up—gives her an excuse to yell at me. She feels needed, and it makes me appreciate how lucky I am to have her. For men and women—that's the circle of life."

Steven considers the idea but still tells Jack, "I don't think married men belong in a private booth. If I want a strip show, I'll buy my wife pole-dancing lessons." His face brightens. "In fact—that's gonna be her Mother's Day gift. Boom—scratch that off the list."

At first I frown at the visual imagery . . . but then get over it and smile. Because I know exactly what to get Kate for *my* birthday.

After Warren emerged from the private booth looking dazed and satisfied—and walking stiffly because he most likely jizzed in his pants—we all sat down front row at the main stage to enjoy another show. This time without my participation. It was a girl-power-themed production, meaning three girls and a variety of battery-powered toys. A show like that is guaranteed to make any man hope for an encore.

I gave it a standing ovation.

Then, the five of us went back to the game room for a dart tournament. See us there? Jack's taking his turn, Steven's watching another member of the Stripper Lollipop Guild play peekaboo with the Blow Pop across the room, while Matthew, Warren, and I lean against the wall nursing our drinks.

Warren's phone pings with an incoming message. He looks down at it for a few seconds and laughs.

For no particular reason, I ask, "What's funny?"

His reaction piques my interest. He drops the hand holding his phone to his side and wipes the grin off his face. "Nothing."

I push off the wall and stand in front of him. "Let me see your phone."

He puts it behind his back. "It's stupid. Nothing you want to see."

"Well, now I fucking do."

Looking like a cornered rat, he calls to Steven, "Reinhart—think fast." And tosses the phone in the air. Steven catches it, but because he always did love a good game of Monkey in the Middle, when I get close to him, he throws it to Matthew. Matthew gets Jack into the game. I take three steps back to Warren, so I'm right in front of him when he catches his phone.

Then I end the game—with a not-too-hard punch to Warren's gut.

Ooomph.

He doubles over, holding his midsection. The phone falls from his hands and clatters to the floor. I pick it up and access the main screen. Warren rasps out, "Evans—I'm telling you as a friend—you shouldn't look at the pictures."

I ignore him.

With the push of a button, the images pop up in all their disgustingly vivid, high-resolution, multi-megapixel splendor. This is a historic day—mark it on your fucking calendar. For once in his life, Warren was right.

I shouldn't have looked.

The guys peer over my shoulder as I scroll through the pictures—clearly from tonight. The first is of Kate on the shoulders of some nameless, bare-chested bastard, surrounded by the outstretched hands of several other dickheads who all bear a strong resemblance to Tarzan. I don't like it, but I can live with it.

The next one shows Kate cradled in the muscular arms of a different thong-wearing prick. Her hands rest on his shoulders, and her skirt has risen up high on her thighs. High enough that, if you look closely, you can spot the pink-and-black-lace panties that caused me so much concern earlier.

I now plan to burn them like toxic waste as soon as we get back to the hotel.

My grip on the phone tightens. If I were a superhero, it'd be dust by now. But I manage to keep my shit together.

Steven comments from behind me, "Buck up, little camper—they're not so bad."

Then I slide to the final image.

Jack says, "Oh, that one's bad."

Bad? Bad is a kid who wipes out on his bike, taking off several layers of skin. *Bad* is Derek Jeter getting sidelined with an injury during the play-offs. This photo isn't bad. It's a blasphemy.

She's leaning back on a dark-upholstered couch, with a guy on top of her—lined up just right to dry-hump her through his black, shiny thong.

If he put her legs on his shoulders, they'd be in one of her favorite positions. And she's smiling. She's looking away from the camera, off to the side, but her mouth is open. Frozen in a wide, laughing scream.

Not exactly the picture of the loyal, devoted fiancée is it?

Every muscle in my body demands that I reach into the device, grab the son of a bitch on top of her, and choke him the fuck out. But the final blow is when I see the writing under the picture. The message Dee-Dee probably gleefully sent. Take a look:

Drew who? :D

Remember what I was saying before? About how when you're in love, the choices you make can have huge effects on the person you love? Well, I wasn't just talking about my choices. I meant Kate's too.

Something inside me cracks. Breaks. Matthew—the only one who senses just how perilously close to the edge I am—tries to pull me back. "It's just a lap dance, dude. It's her bachelorette party. Tomorrow everything goes back to normal."

I laugh and my mouth tastes bitter. My movements are dangerous and desperate. I shove Matthew's hand away and toss Warren's phone back to him.

"You're right, Matthew, it doesn't mean shit. None of it's real, right? It's Cinderella's motherfucking coach, a one-night freebie—then tomorrow, it'll be like it never even happened."

Matthew frowns. "Drew—"

Warren interrupts, "Would you stop being such a fucking hypocrite?" He holds his hands out wide. "Do you see where we are right now?"

I don't think about how he's once again correct. I don't think about all the wrongs I've committed, or all the promises I've made.

Because back in the caveman days? They didn't have time to consider the ramifications of their actions when a woolly mammoth was bearing down on them. All they could do was react. That same primal instinct is pushing me now. Driving me to do something—anything—to get rid of the jealousy that's burning through my chest.

Once upon a time there was a guy, and he was awesome. He had a perfect life—good-looking, a great job, money to burn, and woman tripping over themselves to fuck him. He was the ace in the hole. A number one. Mr. No Apologies, I know exactly what I want and I get it, if you're not with me, you're against me, get on board or get the fuck out.

I liked that guy. He called the shots. He was in control. And there was never a time he felt as bad as I do right now. About anything.

I know what he would've said at a time like this: Stella can lick Chomper's balls; Drew is the one who needs to get his groove back. Then he would've grabbed a stripper and paid for a raunchy lap dance—maybe paid for more. To even the score.

But if you think you know how this goes, you're fucking wrong.

'Cause I'm not going to do *any* of that stuff.

As shitty as this is, as sick and jealous as seeing those pictures makes me feel? I know something that feels even worse.

Letting Kate down. Breaking her trust. Making her cry.

Kate has forgiven me my screwups and she trusts me, even when I don't always give her a reason to. Mercy is a gift—given out of love, not worthiness. And that's what Kate will always be to me.

She's my mercy.

And I will be damned if I punk out and fail to be the man she adores—the man I know I can be. For her. For James.

I rub my eyes and take a breath. The guys watch me as I walk to the bar and sit down.

"What are you going to do?" Warren asks.

"What do you think I'm going to do?"

"Try and make yourself feel better? Hook up with a stripper?" Matthew offers.

I just shrug. "Been there, done that—it never ends well."

Besides, you know as well as I do that she didn't get that lap dance 'cause she wanted it—any more than I wanted a goddamn thong in my mouth. The girls put her up to it, and she was just going with the flow.

Still sucks, though. Which is why when Jack repeats Warren's question, I say, "I'm going to do what any guy in my shoes would do. I'm gonna fucking drink."

The perky bartender appears before me, smiling. "What can I get you, Mr. Evans?"

I shrug. "You got anything that will erase the last five minutes from my brain?"

I meant it as a joke, but she smiles thoughtfully. "Actually, I think I have just what you're looking for."

She walks to the end of the bar and retrieves a long-necked, glittery, sparkling bottle. Someone went a little crazy with the BeDazzler. She holds it up. "This is Pandora. It's part of an in-house contest. Eight hundred dollars a bottle. If you're able to drink the entire contents without passing out, vomiting, or requiring medical intervention, you win an I DOMINATED PANDORA IN PARADISE T-shirt. And we put your name and picture on the Wall of Studs."

She points behind the bar, where WALL OF STUDS is hung on a glowing neon sign. With no pictures underneath.

"If you fail to drink the contents or engage in any of the aforementioned behaviors, your picture and name are relegated to the Wall of Pussies." She gestures to the opposite wall. Where a shitload of pictures hang. Every one featuring some poor slob who's passed out or puking—sometimes both. One guy looks as if he's having a seizure.

I stare at the bottle. "What's in it?"

"Our own blend. I can't tell you the exact proof, but I must warn you, it's quite high. So what do you say, Mr. Evans? Up for the Pandora Challenge?"

Here's a fact for you—men will do practically anything for a T-shirt. Free throws till our backs give out, hot-dog eating until our stomachs rupture. If there's a chance to acquire a cheap cotton garment that proclaims our accomplishment? We're helpless to resist.

"Hell, yeah." I smack the money down on the bar. She hands me the bottle and offers a glass, which I turn down.

I uncork the top and toast the guys. "Party on!"

The liquid is sweet, warm. Not the bitter, burning taste of most hard liquors. I'm sure that I've got this in the bag. Might as well put my T-shirt on right now.

I look at Matthew, who smiles back. "What's the worst that could happen, right?"

Chapter 14

Your body's ability to absorb alcohol and still function depends on several factors: weight, liver health, past patterns of consumption. Most adults already have this figured out, but just in case you're one of those who don't know—I'll tell you. There are different levels of intoxication.

First, there's that warm, happy feeling the average person gets after a drink or two. Most could still operate a car safely and, unless you have a low body mass index, would probably pass a Breathalyzer. We'll call this buzzed.

Then, in the three-to-five-drink range, some people get a little silly. Talkative. Possibly annoying. You're beyond happy at this point, and even the most mundane events seem hilarious. This is often referred to as tipsy.

Next, there's actual drunkenness. By now, you've lost count of the number of drinks you've had. You could bite a hole through your tongue, but you wouldn't feel it. You're slurring your words, and swaying on your feet. We'll call this shitfaced.

The final level of intoxication is completely fucking obliterated. Coherent thought is pretty much gone. Coordination—nonexistent. And your self-awareness equals that of a fruit fly.

About an hour after popping that cork from Pandora's mouth, I am fucking obliterated. Moving is a bit of a challenge. It's similar to those nightmares when the ax murderer is chasing you, and no matter how hard you try, you can't get your legs to move? It feels like a thick, invisible force field of Jell-O is encasing my body—every action is slow and strenuous.

Time has no meaning. Apparently the brain cells are dying off so fucking fast, only short, disjointed moments make it into my actual memory. Like pictures taken with an old Polaroid camera.

As far as I can tell, most of the patrons at Paradise have taken their leave—and my bachelor party has more or less taken over the club.

There's Jack's face, just inches from mine, his mouth open, tongue hanging out, yelling, "Waaaassssuuuuupppppppp?!" There are Steven and Matthew, behind the bar, throwing bottles to one another, pretending to be Tom Cruise doing the Hippy Hippy Shake. There's Warren, getting striptease lessons from a dancer—trying to swing around the pole and falling.

Like that guy needs another blow to the head.

Then there's all of us—onstage—my arm thrown around Warren's shoulder as we belt out "Making Love out of Nothing at All" by Air Supply, while Steven, Matthew, and Jack sing backup.

Christ Almighty.

When the fog clears next, I'm at the bar, my cheek resting sloppily on my hand. Sitting next to me is the dark-haired stripper who rode me onstage. I know I should know her name, but I can't remember it. She's talking animatedly—her hands moving as fast as her mouth. I only hear every third word or so.

I look at the bottle that's on the bar next to me. It's about three-quarters empty. I shrug—bring the bottle to my lips—and just manage to take a drink. A little of the red liquid trickles down my chin and soaks into my shirt. That's embarrassing—I've never been a sloppy drunk.

". . . so, you're okay with that, right, Drew?"

Hearing my name gets my attention, and I turn toward the sound. Like a dog. "Huh?"

She smiles. "I don't usually do this, but you guys are a lot of fun."

I agree. "Yeps . . . tha's usss. We're the GT . . . yeah . . ."

With a compassionate smile, she hops off her barstool. "Take it easy with that stuff, handsome."

I try to hold up two thumbs—the universal sign for *It's all good*—but my fingers don't cooperate. I hold up all ten instead.

She laughs, gives me a high five, and walks away. I sit for a moment. Then—because that's the fucking genius I am—I decide I want to play darts. I drag myself off the bar stool in search of a game.

This won't end well.

Sometime later—could be three hours or thirty minutes—I realize I'm sitting in a chair, at one of the back poker tables. Five cards are in my hand and a stack of chips is next to me.

I can't feel my face—and for a moment, I fear it might have fallen the fuck off. I slap my cheeks.

Still there. *Awesome.*

Across the table, Matthew holds his own cards in his hand. Behind him, a statuesque blonde in a black mesh body stocking is rubbing his shoulders, giving him a massage while he plays. Next to Matthew is Steven. He also has cards in his hand . . . and a hot Asian chick on his lap.

Both seem to be at shitfaced level, so . . . that explains a lot.

On the stage, Billy Warren strums a guitar he must have pulled out of his ass, singing "Mandy" by Barry Manilow.

My phone vibrates, but when I try to fish it out of my pocket, it jumps out of my hands and onto the floor. I push my chair back and get on my knees under the table to look for it. I find the slippery bastard, but when I start to stand back up, my eyes land on the bar.

And there is the one of the most glorious sights I have ever seen.

It's Kate.

She's in jeans and a T-shirt and her back's to me, but I still know—I'm certain—it's her. I'm so fucking relieved, I kind of get a little choked up. I can't explain why, but it feels like it's been so long since I've seen her—goddamn ages. Like so much has happened.

I've missed her. And now she's here.

They must have come here to surprise us. What a great surprise! I pull myself up and stumble forward. I wrap my arms around her from behind, pulling her close against my chest. I bury my face in her neck, in her hair, and breathe her in—enjoying the soothing wonder of being surrounded by all things Kate.

Somewhere, in my Pandora-marinated brain, I recognize that Kate smells . . . different.

Wrong.

But I brush it off. Because I'm too stupidly happy to give a shit about something so trivial.

I lick my lips and put all my energy into not slurring my words as I whisper in her ear, "I'm so glad you're here. Let's just . . . leave. You and me. They won't notice we're gone. I don't care about any of this stuff—I just want to be with you. I want to go back to the hotel and invent new ways to make you come."

My eyes close, and I skim my nose against her cheek. My hand finds Kate's chin and I turn her face toward me. So I can taste her, so I can press my lips to hers and show her how badly I want her—how much I need her.

But before our lips meet . . .

There's a crashing sound in the distance. A commotion. And a Bitchy-sounding voice calls out, "Oh, hell no . . ."

My eyes are still closed, and without warning my equilibrium does a 180. Then I'm falling. Into total darkness.

Chapter 15

Do you see that guy on the bed? The one with the grayish, clammy skin, wearing last night's wrinkled clothes? Nope, it's not a corpse. That's me—Drew Evans.

Not my best look, I admit. But it's the morning after. The time when the piper gets paid. Someone should take my picture—it'd make a great antidrinking billboard. "This is what stupid looks like, kids."

When you think about it, hangovers are kind of interesting. They're your body's way of calling you an asshole. Of saying, "I told you so." You know how I feel. We've all been there. My stomach is rolling, my head is pounding, my mouth is dry, and my breath smells as if I just chowed down on a dog-shit sandwich. *Yum.*

The alarm clock on the nightstand table goes off, music blaring from its speakers, and I'm pretty sure my skull just cracked in two. I roll on my side and breathe out a moan. You don't feel bad for me, do you? I get that. If you want to play, you gotta pay.

Don't do the crime if you can't do the time. Blah, blah, blah. I slap the button on the alarm and the music fades to a low hum.

I open my eyes just enough to see that Kate isn't in the bed next to me. My hand moves across the sheets where she's supposed to be, but they're cold—meaning she's hasn't been here for a while.

I sit up slowly and brace my feet on the floor. My stomach churns like an ocean dinghy during a storm. I rub my temples to try to alleviate the drumming pain. And maybe dislodge a memory. Because I don't know about you—but I don't remember a goddamn thing about last night. It's just . . . blank.

Like a wet sponge on a chalkboard—wiped clean.

Weird. I'm not typically a blackouter. That week Kate left me drowning my sorrows while she hightailed it back to her hometown in Ohio was the only exception. But let's not talk about that.

I guess . . . I shouldn't be surprised. Guys are competitive. Put a bunch of us in a room and we can turn anything into a contest. Who can burp the longest, piss the farthest, whose dick is bigger, who can punch the hardest.

Who can drink the most.

Is that what happened?

I stand stiffly and stumble toward the adjoining bathroom. I open the door. A thick billow of steam floats out. The bathroom's huge—as large as a small bedroom—wall-to-wall Italian marble. The sound of running water echoes from the triple-spouted corner shower.

Behind the blur of the frosted door, I make out the silhouette of a woman—her head tilted back under the spray as she rinses her long, dark hair. She's petite. Skin tanned and toned, with an unmistakably luscious ass.

Technically, I'm still a Catholic—but if you haven't figured it out by now, Kate is my deity. Her body is my holy land, her words are my scripture, her pussy is the altar I'd crawl across burning coals to worship.

My eyes are glued to Kate's hands as they run over her slick skin for a final rinse. I lick my lips and imagine what she tastes like. Clean and wet. Vanilla and lavender. That's all it takes. My southern region rises to attention.

Ten-hut.

It's mind over matter. Or in this case, horniness over hangover. It seems that despite my fragile physical state, the guy downstairs is still cocked and ready for some morning action.

Ha ha . . . cocked . . .

Anyway, I take two steps toward the stall, fully intent on joining my irresistible fiancée. But then the water shuts off. The shower door opens; the dark-haired beauty steps out.

And my heart drops to my feet—like a fucking A-bomb from a World War II fighter plane. Can you hear it whistle?

Big, brown eyes find mine as she reaches for a towel. "Hey, handsome, how are you feeling? You were pretty crazy last night."

She's smiling.

I'm not.

You know how, for some people, just a whiff of peanuts can immediately make their throat close up, cutting off their airway? I don't have a peanut allergy—but now I know how it feels.

They say when you're dying, your life flashes before your eyes. And I can tell you, with all certainty, that they're right. I see images of Kate . . . of our perfect little boy. They flicker in my head like a black-and-white silent movie. They're pictures of the moments we had, of the life we shared.

A life that—without a doubt—is over now. As dead as the goldfish Mackenzie had a few years ago. The one she insisted on bringing to the beach, in her pocket, so he could visit all his fishy friends.

RIP Nemo. *Ashes to ashes, dust to dust.*

I know what you're thinking. What the hell's your problem? Why all the drama? Why is a little naked bush making me go all *Clockwork Orange* bowler-hat psycho?

"Drew? Are you all right?"

The problem, kiddies, is that the beautiful, wet woman standing in front of me—who is obviously well acquainted with me and whatever the hell went down last night?

She's *not* Kate Brooks.

You know that saying, "Pinch me . . . I must be dreaming"? Well, kick me in the balls . . . I'm having a goddamn nightmare.

In a rush it all comes back to me, like a montage on fast-forward. Gambling with the boys, dinner, the fistfight, the thong in my mouth, nuzzling the stripper—Lily—at the bar. But that's all there is. After that last moment, there's nothing but a void.

A black hole—much like the bullet I'm tempted to put right between my fucking eyes at the moment—would leave.

I thought it was her. *Jesus Christ.* I thought it was Kate. When I was embracing her, trying to kiss her—I thought it was Kate.

But it wasn't.

I sit down on the closed toilet lid while Lily wraps a towel around herself—concern lines etched on her face as she watches me. I breathe hard, fast, and my heart beats as if it wants to jump out of my chest and run far, far away from this latest clusterfuck.

What happened? Did the guys pick me up and drag me back to the hotel? I would give my left nut to be able to believe that's how it went down. But if that's the case—why is this girl in my goddamn shower, talking about how crazy I was last night?

Mother . . .

For the first time in my life, I can't think of an appropriate exclamation. Not a curse in existence is powerful enough to fit this situation. Did I sneak out of the bar with her, hijack the limo, and come back here? That sounds like something I could pull off.

Did Kate . . . my stomach twists . . . did Kate *see* us here?

Fucking God Almighty.

My heart picks up even more speed, and I think I may actually be having a heart attack. Is thirty-two too young to have a heart attack? I hope it's not.

Because she's never going to forgive me.

Not this time. All my get-out-of-jail-free cards are used up. I run through every kiss-ass scenario I can think of—every groveling method known to man.

And I discount every single one.

No flower or gift or grand gesture is going to fix this. Hallmark doesn't make an I'M SORRY I NAILED ANOTHER WOMAN, THINKING IT WAS YOU card. Even if I explain . . . Kate will never move past it. Never get over it. Never look or feel about me the same way she did yesterday.

And I don't blame her.

I close my eyes and drop my head into my hands.

She deserves more than this—so much more. Kate deserves someone better than a guy who's going to punch a hole in her soul every two years or so.

Better than me.

"Drew, are you all right? Should I get someone?"

Before I can stutter the questions I don't want to know the answers to, the bathroom door opens. And Billy Warren sticks his head in. His eyes drift from me, to Lily, and back to me. "Everything okay in here?"

"No," she answers. "I think Drew's really sick, boo-boo."

Sick.

That's precisely what I am.

There's something wrong with me. I am messed-up in the head. *You* know it—you probably realized it a long time ago. I keep—

Wait.

Did she just call him *boo-boo*?

Warren walks into the bathroom, stops next to Lily, and puts his hand on my shoulder. "You gotta puke, man? You should—you'll feel better. I told you not to drink that shit last night."

I gaze at Warren's face, trying to remember—to figure out. A tiny flicker of hope sparks in my chest. "Did . . . did you two hook up last night?"

And Douche Bag pisses all over my little flame of hope. "No, we didn't hook up."

Fuck.

But then Shower Girl holds out her left hand and adds giddily, "We got married!"

My head snaps up—and the quick movement makes the pounding return with a sharp vengeance.

Warren straightens and puts an arm around her shoulders—both of them wearing huge, matching grins.

I point between them. "You two . . . you got married?"

He nods. "I figured if Vegas was a good enough place for my cousin to tie the knot, it's good enough for me." His gaze shifts to Lily adoringly. "When you find someone this amazing—when you know it's the real thing—you don't let it pass you by."

I squint. "Married?"

Lily nods enthusiastically. "At the Drive-Through Wedding Chapel. We took some great pictures. And now I'm Mrs. Billy Warren."

Nope, still can't wrap my head around it. "Married? Really?"

Warren's expression goes from sappy to annoyed. "Yeah, Long Duck Fuckin' Dong—married. What's your problem?"

It finally sinks in. Donkey Dick married Shower Girl. But more important:

I. Didn't. Screw her.

Cue the chorus of angels. *Ahhh-le-luia, ahhh-le-luia, alleluia, alleluia, ah-leee-luia . . .*

I *didn't* mess up. I didn't betray Kate or ruin our son's life or destroy everything we have. Overcome with emotion, I may actually weep with relief.

But I don't cry. I do something much, much worse. I stand up and hug Billy Warren. "I love you, man."

Yes, the stress of the last few minutes has finally driven me over the edge. We embrace for a second before he pushes me back, holds me at arm's length, and looks at me with confused brown eyes.

"Dude," he utters disgustedly.

I come to my senses. And shake my muddled head. "Sorry, I just . . . I'm so happy for you."

Translation? I'm over-fucking-joyed for *me*. And that he married a woman who looks freakishly identical to Kate?

Nope—don't even care.

I give his back a congratulatory smack. "You and . . ." I . . . pat her head. "Both of you. Congratulations."

Then I realize I still have no idea where the hell Kate is. I hook my thumb toward the door. "I gotta go."

As fast as my feet can carry me, I dash out the door.

Stepping out of the bedroom into the living area feels similar to when Dorothy stepped out of her dilapidated house into Oz. Everything is too bright, too colorful . . . too loud.

Matthew and Delores sit close together on the couch, under a beige blanket, sharing a bowl of cereal and watching *Gilligan's Island* on TV. Matthew chuckles at the television before Dee feeds him a scoop of Froot Loops.

As I step into the room, Matthew's attention turns to me. "You're alive."

Delores is disappointed. "Damn it. I was hoping we'd have to get your stomach pumped."

Matthew tugs her strawberry-blond ponytail and tells her firmly, "I told you to be nice from now on. Cut that shit out."

When he turns back to me, Delores sticks her tongue out at him.

The ecstatic adrenaline rush from learning I did not actually put my dick in a pussy that wasn't Kate's is starting to wear off. My head and stomach resume the nauseating symphony of a mighty hangover.

I rub my temples and inform Matthew and Dee, "You know Billy got married last night?"

In unison, they respond wearily, "Yep."

"To a stripper he's known for less than twenty-four hours?"

"Yep."

Though I think I already know the answer, I ask the third-stupidest question ever: "Did he get her to sign a prenup?"

Delores scoffs, "I'm not sure my cousin knows how to spell *prenup*."

Thump.

Thump.

They seem way too calm about this development. "Why didn't you stop him?"

Now Dee glares at me. "Are you fucking kidding me?"

Matthew explains, "Drew, it was your idea."

My face goes slack. "It was?"

"It was. After you woke up from your nosedive at the strip club, you went on and on about how great marriage is. How everyone should get fucking married. How love is a precious, beautiful flower, and marriage is the water and sunlight that helps it grow."

I seriously need to never drink again. *Ever.*

"I said that?"

Matthew nods. "You were very poetic."

"Shit. We should call Wilson—he's the best divorce lawyer in New York City." And an old colleague of my mother's. "Maybe he can draft something that'll work retroactively."

Matthew takes another bite of cereal. "Already left him a message."

Thump.

Thump.

My fingers move from my temples to my forehead, continuing to rub the torturous pounding. "What else am I missing?"

"What's the last thing you remember?" Matthew asks.

"Um . . . playing poker with you and Steven at Paradise. Warren singing Barry Manilow onstage."

My best friend laughs. "You're missing a lot." He sets the bowl of cereal down on the coffee table and elaborates. "Kate, Dee, Lexi, and Erin decided to crash our party and showed up at Paradise. After we left the police station—"

I cut him right off. "Why were we at the police station?"

"Because that's where they take you when you get arrested."

"We got arrested?"

He grins. "Oh, no—*we* didn't get arrested."

Dee raises her hand. "*We* did."

My eyes go wide. "Kate was in jail?"

Thump.

Matthew waves his hand calmly. "Only for, like, twenty minutes. They released the girls to our custody—no charges were filed. I smoothed things over with the strip club."

Going with the usual-suspect line of thought, I turn on Delores. "What did you do to get Kate arrested?"

She just laughs. "You can thank your sister for that one—Alexandra didn't appreciate her husband getting so much attention from the strippers. When one of them got in her face, Lexi showed her what was up—and the rest of us had her back. I'll say this much: for a trust-fund baby, the Bitch has got a mean right hook."

This is not news to me.

"Jesus Christ," I sigh. "All right, forget all that—just tell me where Kate is."

Dee looks confused. "What do you mean? She's in your room."

Thump.

Before I can point out that Kate is not, in fact, in our room, one of the bedroom doors opens. Erin steps out, wrapped in a fluffy bathrobe, her hair wet. "Good morning, everyone!"

"Hey, naughty girl," Dee greets her.

Erin steps into the kitchen. "Mmm . . . coffee."

And prepare to have your mind blown—because in the bedroom doorway Erin just exited appears none other than . . . Jack O'Shay.

Shirtless. Wearing only boxers.

No way.

He stretches his arms wide above his head with a yawn, then scratches his chest and adjusts his balls. "What a great fucking night, huh? I'm actually sad you're only getting married once, Evans. I could definitely do that again."

Please look closely at my face. Did my eyeballs fall out of my head? 'Cause it feels like they have.

I look at Matthew. He just nods and flicks his hand, silently telling me, *What are you gonna do?*

Thump.

Thump.

Thump.

As Erin sticks her head into the refrigerator behind us, Jack stands next to me. In a low voice I ask, "Did you . . . is this . . ."

"Is this what you think it is?" He grins like a well-fed feline. "It is, and I did." Then, softer, he says, "Erin's a wildcat, man. Easily made the top three bangs of my lifetime. I'll fill you in later."

If this ends up causing Erin to not be my secretary in the near future—I'm going to have to kill Jack. Seriously. I can always find more friends. Finding a secretary who knows her shit as well as Erin does? That'll be much more difficult.

Erin comes back into the room sipping her coffee. Jack grabs a newspaper off the table and announces, "I'll be in the john." Before he goes, he adds, "Hey, Erin—how about you bring me a cup of coffee for when I get out?"

Erin smiles sweetly. "Hey, Jack—how about you get it yourself? This isn't the office, and even if it was, I don't work for you."

Jack just chuckles and goes back into the bedroom.

Thump.

I turn to stare at Erin. My voice is teasingly aghast as I say, "Erin. I am *shocked.* I can't believe you let Jack play you—I thought you were smarter than that."

She clears her throat. "Did you ever consider the possibility that *I'm* the one who played *Jack*?"

I touch my jaw thoughtfully because, no, I hadn't considered that.

Thump.

Erin continues, "I came here hoping to meet Mr. Right, but he didn't appear. Jack is cute, and, more important, he was ready, willing, and able. You do the math."

"But isn't that going to be weird for you, working in the same office every day? He's seen your cum face." I pause. "At least . . . I hope he's seen your cum face."

Erin winks. "He's well acquainted with it." She sips her coffee. "But, no, it's not going to be awkward. We're adults—and what happens in Vegas stays in Vegas, right?"

"I guess so."

Unless you're Billy Warren. In his case, what happens in Vegas may end up taking 50 percent of his net worth.

With that, Erin goes back to the kitchen, pours a second cup of coffee, and returns to the bedroom Jack retreated to, closing the door behind her.

I shake my head a little. "Wow."

I'm about to ask Matthew and Dee where Kate is again—but that rhythmic knocking noise starts back up. Do you hear it too?

Thump.

Thump.

Thump.

"What the hell is that noise?"

Like those disturbing twins from *The Shining*, my best friend and his wife answer in harmony yet again. "Steven and Alexandra."

The racket does seem to be coming from behind their closed door. "What are they, nailing each other to a cross?"

Matthew mutters, "Something's getting nailed all right."

Thump.

Cautiously, I step toward their door. When I'm inches away, I align my ear with the seam at the hinge. Listening.

"Who's your daddy, baby? Say it, say my name."

"Steven, ooohhh, Steven."

Then the unmistakable sound of a palm slapping ass reaches my ear.

"Ahhh!" I jump back away from the door as if it were an electrified fence. I cover my ears, but it's too late.

I bend over and brace my hands on my knees, on the verge of actually vomiting. I just hope the villa is stocked with hydrogen peroxide, so I can sterilize my eardrums.

After the desire to upchuck passes, I stand up and address Dee and Matthew. "Screw all this. The only thing I want to know is—where. Is. Kate?"

Delores answers, "I told you, dumbass, she's in your room. We tucked you two into bed together as soon as we came back last night."

"I was just in our room! She's not there!"

Delores shrugs. "Maybe she decided to bail on the wedding—pried open the window and made a break for it." Then she smiles. "If that's the case—good on her."

Matthew pulls Dee's hair again, but says, "It's true, Drew; Kate hasn't left the room—we would've seen her." He turns back to his wife and warns, "If yanking your hair doesn't get the job done, I'm going to break out the paddle."

She leans closer and taunts, "Promises, promises." Then she kisses him, ignoring my dilemma completely. I push my hand through my hair, then turn away and march back to our bedroom.

My eyes scan the bed, but Kate's not there. Just to be safe, I pick up the blanket and shake it out.

Nothing.

I enter the walk-in closet next to the bedroom door. Though I realize it's unlikely, I check behind the hanging clothes. Not a sign of Kate to be seen. Then I walk out of the closet and take a few steps around the bed . . .

On the floor, peeking out from the far side of the bed, are five pretty toes. They're connected to a beautiful foot. My eyes travel from the foot, up the delectable calf, to the exquisite thigh that fits so perfectly around my hip.

Still in last night's clothes, sound asleep on her side, one leg stretched out, one tucked close to her torso, with folded hands resting under her cheek, like a pillow.

Kate.

Every cell in my body sighs her name with relief. I stand there for a minute, just watching her—breathing in the sight of her as she slumbers like a kitten in front of a fireplace. The all-encompassing love I have for her, that's always with me—I feel it more keenly. Because even for just a few minutes, I'd thought I hurt her.

I grab a pillow and the blanket and drop to my knees beside Kate. Then I lie on the makeshift floor bed and gather her tight against me. My chest pillows her head.

She stirs with a moan. "Drew?"

I smooth her hair. "Yeah, baby, it's me."

Without lifting her head, she wonders in a drowsy voice, "Why are you on the floor?"

I kiss the top of her head and whisper against her hair, "Because that's where you are."

After a pause, she just says, "Oh."

My hand slides up and down her back, her arm, savoring every touch—enjoying the feel of her next to me. "Did you have fun last night?"

Still lying on my chest, she nods. "Uh-huh." Then Kate breathes deep and suggests, "Let's never do anything like this again."

"I could not agree with that statement more."

We're quiet for a few moments. I look up at the ceiling, wanting and needing to get a few more hours of sleep. But I have to tell her one more thing first.

"Kate?" I squeeze her shoulder gently. "Hey, Kate?"

"Mmmm?"

My voice is low, rough with emotion, as I confess, "I really can't wait to marry you."

She raises her head and gazes at me with adorable bleary eyes. She smiles. "Yeah . . . me too."

Kate lays her head back down, and her hand rests right over my heart. I cover her hand with mine, and together we fall back to sleep.

Epilogue

So what have we learned from this story?

First and foremost, bachelor parties?

Terrible idea.

Once you're in a committed relationship, going to bars or a strip club without your significant other is just asking for trouble. Whoever started the bachelor-party tradition should be buried alive in a mass grave with the karaoke guy and . . . well . . . I was going to say Billy Warren.

But I guess we can let him live. I'm over it—he's harmless. He's also dim-witted, annoying, and . . . decent . . . a stand-up guy, a good friend.

You already knew that, didn't you?

We'll never be the best of friends, but from here on out, the one or two times a year I have to see him will actually be okay with me.

What else?

Have faith in yourself—it actually is possible to learn from your mistakes. I did. And this time, when I was on the spot, I didn't screw up. I believed in Kate, trusted what we have, and did the right thing. *Fucking finally.*

Now let's get to the part you've been waiting for:

The wedding.

Matthew, Jack and Steven, my parents, James and I, arrive at St. Patrick's Cathedral right on time. Although they rarely close the church to the public, for our event—and to accommodate the thousand-plus guests sitting in the pews—the powers that be agreed to do just that. The hefty "donation" I gave didn't hurt either.

I keep an eye on my son as he runs up and down the aisle, stopping occasionally to bask in the attention of an adoring guest. Then I shake hands with Father Dougherty, the priest who'll actually be doing the deed.

"How are you feeling this afternoon, Andrew? Are you ready?"

"I was born ready, Father."

"That's good to hear. Your bride's limousine has just arrived, so you can take your place at the altar."

There's no anxiety—no nervousness or fear that I'm making a mistake. No cold feet. The only thing I feel is . . . excitement. Impatience.

My mother retrieves James and they head back to the vestibule. My father and I walk up the side aisle, toward the altar.

About halfway there, he stops me with a hand on my shoulder. His blue eyes, so much like my own, are filled with emotion.

"If I haven't told you before, I want to make sure you know—I'm so proud of you, Son. You're a good man, you're an amazing father, and I have no doubt you'll be an outstanding husband. I'm so very proud, Drew."

Then he hugs me. Tight and secure, the kind of embrace that tells me even though I'm married and a father—he's still my dad and I'll always be his son.

"That means a lot, Dad," I say gruffly. "Thank you for being the best example of what a father, a husband, is supposed to be."

We pat each other's back. Then he taps my biceps. "Now get up there before Kate changes her mind."

I smirk. "Highly unlikely."

He shrugs. "Better to be safe than sorry. I didn't think your mother would try backing out, either."

Haven't heard that one before. "Mom balked at marrying you?"

He slaps my back again. "That's a story for another day, Son. Go get yourself married—and enjoy every second of it."

With that, he walks to the back of the church. I meet Matthew and Steven at the altar. "You got the rings?" I ask Matthew.

He taps his pocket. "Safe and sound."

When the pianist begins playing the prelude—"Angels Watching" by the O'Neill Brothers—Steven announces, "That's our cue."

Matthew grins my way and imitates the Terminator: "I'll be back." They both walk down the side aisle to the back of the church.

I'm left standing alone. Waiting.

I nod to the watching guests. One hand rests at my side, the other is folded across my lower back. I inhale a deep breath and blow it out slowly.

The string quartet in the orchestra bay begins to play Canon in D by Pachelbel.

It's game time.

The first to appear in the doorway are our parents. My father looks distinguished as he stands in the middle, my mother, wearing a plum gown, on one arm; Kate's mother, in deep blue, is on the other. All three wear beaming smiles as they proceed down the aisle. Before my mother enters the pew, she blows me a kiss. She used to do the same thing when I was a kid, as I ran out the door to school—before I was old enough to ask her to stop.

I smile back at her meaningfully.

Next are my sister and Steven. Alexandra looks gorgeous in the strapless, burgundy bridesmaid gown Kate chose. An ivory shawl demurely covers her shoulders: her blond hair is pinned up and curled, not a strand out of place. Her arm rests comfortably, confidently, through Steven's. They glance at each other and I just know they're thinking of their own wedding. When they reach the altar, Steven kisses Lexi sweetly, then they part and stand on their respective sides.

Jack and Erin follow, arm in arm. Jack winks at a female guest as he strolls down the aisle and Erin smiles joyfully. Brightly. If you ever wanted a good example of how a no-strings-attached hookup should be done, Jack and Erin are it. No bad feelings, no awkwardness, just friendly, physical attraction.

After they reach the altar, it's Matthew and Dee-Dee's turn—the best man and matron of honor. Wearing the same gown as my sister—instead of one of the whacked-out ensembles she typically dresses in—Delores looks really good. She holds Matthew's arm and sways her hips in time with the music, making him laugh at her silly exuberance. When they reach the altar, she looks me up and down—then gives me a thumbs-up.

I nod at her silent compliment.

Delores stands beside my sister, and Matthew takes his place to my left.

One more couple to go before Kate makes her entrance. This couple will steal the whole fucking show. I knew it, Kate knew it, and neither of us minded at all.

Mackenzie and James.

The flower girl and the ring bearer. The gold mine of every wedding photographer who ever worked.

Mackenzie's dress is white lace with cap sleeves. Her long hair is pulled up at the sides with white daisies woven into the crown of blond braids. She's old enough to be called beautiful but still enough of a kid to be called adorable. Her blue eyes shine as she waves to me from the end of the aisle.

I wave back.

She takes my son's hand and together they make their way to me. James looks impressively lovable in his own custom Armani tux. He's surprisingly well behaved—keeping pace with Mackenzie, holding his ring-bearer pillow straight, grinning for all the cameras taking their picture.

When they reach the altar, James drops Mackenzie's hand, ditches his pillow, and runs straight to me. "Daddy!"

I scoop him up and look into his big, brown eyes.

"Is good?" he asks.

"You did great, buddy." I kiss his temple. "Go sit with Grandma and Pop now, okay?"

"Otay."

I set him down and my parents receive him into their pew.

Then I straighten up. The starting notes of the "Wedding March" fill the cathedral. All the guests stand and turn toward the closed double doors.

The wooden doors open. And the air rushes from my lungs.

Because she's breathtaking. More stunning than I'd imagined—and my imagination is pretty fucking active.

Kate's a vision in white—strapless, a sweetheart neckline with just a teasing taste of cleavage, fitted around the middle, accenting her tiny waist. Lace covers the delicate swell of her hips, flaring out behind her in a majestic train. An Irish-lace veil adorns her head, and her hair falls in shiny, dark waves beneath it. Her makeup is light, just enough to emphasize her flawless skin, full lips, and those big, dark eyes that captivated me the moment I saw them.

She swallows hard and gazes around the crowded cathedral, looking uneasy. Anxious. Until she sees me. At the altar—waiting for her.

She holds my eyes for a second, then slowly, surely, she smiles.

And it's perfect.

My view of the world blurs, and I don't give a shit if that sounds pussified. It's true. And deserved. My chest tightens with tenderness, with the sanctity of this moment.

The music soars as Kate holds George's arm, and he escorts her down the aisle. I can't take my eyes off her, and her gaze never leaves my face. When they finally arrive, I shake George's hand and he moves into the pew next to Carol.

Kate offers me her hand, and, as I did the first time we met, I bring it to my lips and kiss it reverently.

"You're exquisite," I tell her softly. "I . . . have no words."

Her smile doesn't falter. "I guess there really is a first time for everything."

It's as if everyone else, the whole damn church, just fades away. And there's only the two of us. I cup her cheek and smooth her lip with my thumb. Then I lean forward and kiss her—softly and slowly and brimming with feeling.

After a few seconds, Father Dougherty clears his throat. Loudly. "That part comes later, son."

I end the kiss and turn to the priest, still holding Kate's hand.

Kate blushes and the guests' laughter echoes off the walls.

I clear my throat. "Sorry, Father. Patience has never really been my strong suit."

"Well, in this case, I don't blame you." He focuses on Kate. "You look lovely."

"Thank you, Father." She passes her bouquet of white daisies and roses to Delores.

"Shall we get on with it, then?" Father Dougherty asks.

From the first row, James yells, "Ready, set, go!"

Again, laughter ripples through the congregation.

Father Dougherty says, "I'll take that as a yes."

The wedding ceremony proceeds without incident—the prayers, the readings, the lighting of the unity candle. Then the moment you've all been waiting for arrives.

Father Dougherty asks, "Andrew, do you promise to be true to Katherine in good times and bad, in sickness and health? Do you promise to love, honor, and cherish her until death do you part?"

In a clear voice, I pledge, "I sure do."

Kate's eyes hold mine and her smile is so bright—so true—as Father Dougherty asks her, "And do you, Katherine, promise to be true to Andrew in good times and bad, in sickness and health? Do you promise to love, honor, and cherish him until death do you part?"

Tears well in her beautiful brown eyes. "Yes. Yes, I do."

It takes everything I've got not to pull her to me and kiss her again.

Matthew passes me the rings and Kate holds out her hand.

My throat tightens as I place her ring on her finger. "I give you this ring as a token of my love and devotion. I pledge to you all that I am, all I'll ever be. With this ring, I marry you and join my life to yours."

Kate holds my hand for an extra moment. Then, tears slip down her cheeks as she slides my own ring on my finger, saying in a voice choked with emotion, "I give you this ring as a token of my love and devotion. I pledge to you all that I am and all that I will ever be. With this ring, I gladly marry you and join my life to yours."

Then Father Dougherty declares, "I now pronounce you husband and wife. What God has joined together, let no man pull asunder. You may kiss your bride."

Without hesitation, I sweep Kate up into my arms. She laughs and wraps her arms around my neck, and our mouths fuse hot and heavy. The kiss is long and thorough and totally inappropriate for church.

Applause and whistles erupt, the church bells ring, and the musicians belt out "Ode to Joy."

Finally, reluctantly, I set Kate on her high-heeled feet and we walk down the aisle side by side.

Hand in hand.

Husband and wife.

We take a thousand fucking pictures, in a variety of locations and every conceivable combination. James holds up like a trouper—

doesn't get cranky once. The photographer had to ask Kate and me to stop making out so we could smile for the camera. Apparently, my hand on her ass is *not* an acceptable pose for a wedding portrait.

But I think he's just flat-out wrong about that.

Once we all pile into the limo, Matthew passes me a bottle of champagne. I pop the cork, spewing bubbles everywhere. Some splashes on my face, and Kate leans over and slowly licks it off.

Delores whistles.

"Mmm . . . ," Kate hums to me. "Champagne tastes good on you, Mr. Evans."

I laugh. "I can think of a few other spots it'll taste even better, Mrs. Evans."

She giggles. "Make sure we have a bottle in the honeymoon suite tonight, then."

"Way ahead of you, baby." Her body puts Waterford crystal to shame.

I fill glasses and pass them around the limo. Steven gives Mackenzie a sip from his, and her face scrunches up adorably with disgust.

James climbs onto his mother's lap and rests his head against her chest.

Kate strokes his dark hair. "He's not going to last."

I take a drink from my glass. "The way you look in that dress? Neither am I."

"I thought your favorite dress was the one I'm not wearing?"

"This one is the exception. Although, I should reserve judgment until I see you out of it." I kiss her ear, then whisper into it, "After a long, exhaustive perusal . . . I'll make my preference abundantly clear."

She gazes at me tenderly, with soft adulation shining on her beautiful face. "I'm so happy, Drew."

Mission accomplished.

"Me too."

I stroke James's back and pull Kate close with my free arm. She nuzzles my neck and rests her cheek against my collarbone. With our friends' raucous laughter all around us, we savor the moment.

The limo pulls up to the Four Seasons, where our reception is being held. Matthew climbs out first, then helps Dee, who brings her glass of champagne with her. James, recharged after his mommy-cuddle, bounds out next, followed by Mackenzie, Alexandra, and Steven. When the driver offers his hand to Kate, I tip him and say, "I got this, thanks."

Then I assist my wife out of the limousine.

My wife.

I don't think I'll ever get tired of thinking of her that way. I'm definitely gonna be looking for excuses to speak of her that way.

I escort her under the twinkling lighted archway into the building where we'll celebrate our marital bliss. Though you and I both know the real celebration happens in the honeymoon suite.

Our group arrives at the well-appointed suite adjacent to the main ballroom, where the wedding party enjoys the cocktail hour away from the prying eyes of the guests—like rock stars in the greenroom. Lauren Laforet, our wedding planner, greets us, makes sure we're good so far, then walks off dictating orders into a walkie-talkie to her minions. Delores and Alexandra have Kate stand to "bustle" the back of her dress, so she can dance without getting stepped on and falling on her face.

I don't know what the "bustle" entails, but by the look of concentration on their faces—I don't want any part of it. I head over to the buffet and pile hors d'oeuvres onto a plate for Kate.

Gotta keep her strength up for later.

While she stands, I feed her piece by piece. I'm guessing she didn't eat this morning because she moans and sighs with each mouthwatering bite. Or maybe she just likes sucking on my fingers—'cause she does that too.

With a knowing smirk, Kate asks me, "You're enjoying this, aren't you?"

My semistiff dick nods. "Immensely." I slide a small, bacon-wrapped scallop between her lips, and her tongue swirls around my finger.

"So am I."

Called it. "Suck it harder," I tell her—only half joking.

She obliges.

When I reach for another piece, Kate says, "Now, where have I heard that before?"

"Get used to hearing it more. There's a good chance it'll be my mantra for the next three weeks."

"Hello," Alexandra calls from where she's crouched behind Kate. "We can hear you. And . . . ewwww."

"Yet you'll still never be as damaged as I was by what I heard from your fucking room in Vegas."

The peroxide didn't work. Sometimes, late at night, I can still hear them.

I'm considering therapy. Or hypnosis.

She just grins slyly. "That was a great morning."

"What was a great morning?" Steven asks, as he brings my sister a cocktail.

She looks at Steven the way a twelve-year-old looks at a Justin Bieber poster. "Every morning with you."

He kisses her lips.

I catch Mackenzie's eye from across the room, wink, and tilt my head toward her parents. She beams back at me, and I know things at home have been back on track with Lexi and Steven. Then Mackenzie mouths, *So gross.*

I just nod.

After the food, music is the second most important ingredient for a successful wedding reception. We hired a twelve-piece band, and a DJ for the songs that just sound stupid when someone other than the original artist covers them. The wedding singer—a voluptuous redhead with stellar pipes—introduces us as Mr. and Mrs. Drew Evans for the first time, and as our guests stand and applaud, I lead Kate to the dance floor for the customary first dance.

It's the wedding singer's partner—a salt-and-pepper-haired guy with a smooth voice—who sings it. Kate, being more musically inclined than I'll ever be, chose the song—but I got final approval.

"I Cross My Heart" by George Strait.

The lyrics, the tone, it's perfect for us.

And just like in the church, while we waltz around the dance floor and I hold her close against me, the thousand eyes watching us fade from our awareness. It's just me and her—and this moment.

I look into my wife's shining brown eyes, and I sing the lyrics to her that mean the most:

You will always be the miracle that makes my life complete.

Kate sings the next line back to me:

And as long as there's a breath in me, I'll make yours just as sweet.

It's a sickeningly tender, crazy-in-love, never-happens-in-real-life kind of moment that I would've made fun of if I saw it in a movie or on TV.

But because it's real—because it's us—it's fucking impeccable.

Afterward, Kate dances with my father to "The Way You Look Tonight" by Frank Sinatra. The old man's a great dancer, and he makes Kate smile and laugh. At one point she gets choked up from whatever words he's whispering to her, and I make a mental note to ask her later on what he said.

Then my mother and I take the floor—Kenny Rogers, "Through the Years." Her eyes fill with tears as she looks at me.

"Don't cry, Mom."

She laughs self-depreciatingly. "I can't help it. You're my little boy and I'm so happy for you, Drew."

Mothers are the first woman a man will ever love—at least the good ones are. They show you how a lady should and shouldn't be treated, and they set the standard for every woman that comes after them. I really lucked out in that department.

My mother continues, "She's your match in every way. You chose so well."

I glance at Kate, who stands beside her mother and George—so goddamn lovely, it makes my heart ache.

"Yeah, I really did, didn't I?" I kiss my mother's cheek. "Thank you, Mom. If it wasn't for you—I never would've been able to win over a woman like Kate."

My mother hugs me as we finish the dance. No more words are needed.

After that, the party really gets started. The lights are turned down low, accenting the tall, candlelit centerpieces, overflowing with white blossoms. We drink, we laugh, we devour amazing culinary delights. Once Kate and I have managed to chat with every one of our guests and thank them for joining us on our "special day," a couple approaches us.

Billy Warren and his stripper-heeled, tiny-black-dress-wearing wife.

Yep, they're still married—six whole days now. That's a hell of a lot longer than I was betting on. I shake Warren's hand. "Good to see you." I turn to his dark-haired companion. "And with clothes on. Even better."

I told Kate all about the hangover-shower meet-and-greet. She thought it was hysterical.

Warren smiles. "You mind if I borrow your wife for a dance?"

Because he called her my wife, I don't mind at all. "As long as you give her back."

Kate kisses my cheek and heads off with Hopeless.

His blushing bride goes to the bar. I stand alone, watching the swaying couples on the dance floor. Until Matthew comes up, arms crossed, standing next to me, taking it all in.

He nods toward Kate and Warren. "You okay with that?"

"Strangely enough, I really am."

We're silent for a beat. Maybe it's just the significance of the day, but I'm feeling pretty fucking sentimental. "Have I ever thanked you for being my best friend?"

Matthew smiles. "No thanks are needed. It's a mutually beneficial thing we've got going on."

"Yeah, but . . . thank you for pulling my ass out of the fire—and for kicking it when needed. Or at least . . . getting Alexandra to do your dirty work for you. I don't know what I'd do without you, man."

"I feel the same way." Then he spreads his arms wide. "Let's hug it out, bitch."

I laugh, and we do just that, slapping each other on the back.

Until Delores comes tearing up to us, holding the knife that we're soon supposed to cut the cake with.

"You son of a bitch!"

Something tells me she's not talking to Matthew.

"I'm gonna stab you in your scrotum!"

This sounds serious.

As Matthew restrains his wife, I ask calmly, "Is there a reason you have the sudden urge to sexually mutilate me?"

She tells her husband, "Helga just called. Documents were delivered to the house that she had to sign for. Legal documents—he changed our son's name, Matthew!"

Damn it. Those weren't supposed to arrive until Kate and I were on our honeymoon—far away, in the middle of the Mediterranean for three wonderful, naked weeks.

Matthew looks over his shoulder at me. "Seriously?"

I throw my arms up in the air. "You'll thank me one day. And so will Michael."

Delores lifts the knife.

"If I didn't love you two and your son, I wouldn't bother." I let that sink in a minute. "And you're one to talk—what about that text you sent Billy from the bachelorette party? If I wasn't so evolved, that could've really fucked things up for me and Kate. And . . . it hurt my feelings."

Did it really? No. But you play the cards you're dealt.

My admission calms Dee a little. I have a feeling she and Matthew have already discussed it. "That was a joke, Drew. If I really hated you . . . I wouldn't put any effort into torturing you. I'd just ignore you completely."

Matthew interjects, "We'll change his name back. It was a screwed-up attempt at a nice gesture, but we'll change it back."

I doubt they will. And if they do . . . I'll just have to be stealthier in my next attempt.

Kate comes over, looking only half-concerned. But she still stands in front of me protectively.

"Dee-Dee? Remember we said no bloodshed on the wedding day—it's bad luck."

Dee sighs and tosses the knife on the table. "I need a drink."

Matthew nods. "I'll join you."

After they're gone, Kate turns around to me. "The papers arrived early, didn't they?"

"They did."

She shakes her head. "I told you it was a bad idea."

I wrap my arms around her because she's gorgeous when she's right. "I should've listened to you."

She smiles up at me. "Maybe we should have kept 'obey' in the vows."

She does have a point.

We dance. Slow and sweet, dirty and sweaty. At one point, while I'm grinding against Kate's ass, James barrels onto the dance floor with Sister Beatrice Dugan hot on his heels. I pick him up, and the first nun I ever lusted after smiles with appreciation.

"Are you enjoying your celebration, Katherine?"

"I am, Sister, very much."

"I'll be praying for you both—for a long and fruitful union."

I bounce James and he squeals. "All our prayers have been answered, Sister B—save yours for someone who really needs them."

She clicks her tongue. "All newlyweds need the Lord's grace, Andrew."

Disgruntled with not being the center of attention, James rectifies the situation. "Poosy!" he yells, laughing manically. "Poosy!"

I freeze, and Kate's eyes slide closed.

Sister B smirks. "And this darling seems to have his father's disposition."

Kate opens her eyes. "Very much so, yes."

Sister B pats Kate's arm with sympathy. "Then I'll be praying doubly hard." She addresses our son. "Would you like a soda pop, young James?"

His eyes widen and he nods quickly. I put him down, and, holding Sister B's hand, he toddles off.

The music changes to a slower song—"All of Me" by John Legend. Without a word, Kate raises her arms to my shoulders, I rest my hands on her lower back, and we sway in time to the beat.

That's when I notice another couple dancing off to my

right—not anywhere as close as Kate and I are—but still, for a second I'm shocked.

Because it's Mackenzie and Johnny Fucking Fitzgerald.

Her one hand is on his shoulder, his at her waist, while their other arms are bent at the elbow, hands clasped in the classic ballroom posture.

I almost pity him. Because even though it's not intentional? My girl was born to be a heartbreaker.

As I watch them silently, Johnny makes his move. Catching Mackenzie off guard, the little bastard presses his lips to hers and snatches a kiss. Her first, I'm guessing. It's chaste and over as quickly as it started.

Johnny pulls back and looks hopeful. But Mackenzie . . . she seems confused . . . until she's not. Then she rips her hand from his.

And punches him right in the gut.

"Ooof!" He folds at the waist, holding his stomach, and Mackenzie stomps off.

I help the kid off the dance floor. "You need to work on reading a chick's signals or you're gonna be getting hit a lot, Casanova."

"Kenzie hits hard for a girl," he rasps.

"She kicks harder. You got off lucky." Once he's in a chair, I pat his shoulder. "Better luck next time."

Then I return to my wife's waiting arms.

An hour later, it's speech time. Completely at ease, Matthew taps his glass with a spoon and then addresses the silenced crowd.

"As the best man, I could stand up here and tell you stories about Drew and Kate. How they met, their accomplishments and battles at the office, what amazing parents they are, how devoted they are to family and friends. But that would take a long time . . . and dessert is coming." The audience chuckles. "So I'll sum it up like this: Drew is one of a kind in the greatest of ways. When God made him, he broke the mold. But he didn't want him to be alone. So he made Kate, and then he broke her mold too." Matthew raises his glass and the crowd raise theirs. "If ever there was a man and a woman who were perfect for each other, who deserve each other and bring out the best in each other—it's you two. Congratulations on your marriage—may it be long and fun and frisky—and may you always look at one another the way you do today. To Drew and Kate."

Got to hand it to him—Matthew knows how to give a good fucking speech.

After toasting us, the crowd calls for a kiss—which I'm more than happy to provide.

Later, after Delores got wasted and dragged Kate and Billy onstage to sing "That's What Friends Are For," after the cake was cut and I licked the icing off Kate's lips, after Kate threw her bouquet into Erin's waiting arms, and Dee's stepbrother made a diving catch of the garter, we dance the final dance.

The floor is packed with our family, with all of our friends. In the center are me and Kate. I hold a sleeping James with one arm, his head on my shoulder. The other arm is around Kate's waist, holding her tight against me, her head on my chest, my lips resting against her hair.

If you've got a camera, I'd whip it out right about now—'cause that's the money shot. The picture you're going to want to remember.

My parents take James to their room for the night. Kate and I fly out tomorrow afternoon. While we're gone, James will stay a week with my sister and Steven, and a week with Matthew and Dee. Then, my parents will bring him out to us on the Amalfi Coast in Italy. They'll take off on their own romantic getaway, and Kate, James, and I will enjoy the last leg of the honeymoon together.

The elevator opens on the top floor. Before Kate steps out, I sweep her into my arms and cradle her as I walk to our suite.

"You're supposed to carry me over the threshold, Drew. Not through the whole hotel."

I shrug. "I've always been an overachiever."

I open the door and carry her in. The bed is awesome. An oversize king with huge, fluffy pillows, red silk sheets, and a comforter of the softest down. Rose petals are scattered in a path to the bed and over the covers, giving off a soft but fragrant scent.

I shift Kate in my arms and slide her down my body. Her eyes dance with happy mischief as they look into mine. "I'm going to need some help getting out of this dress."

I crack my knuckles. "You've got the right man for the job."

My fingers ghost along the silky skin of her back. I take my time with the buttons, popping each one slowly, giving Kate's imagination time to run wild.

As the last button is released, I step closer to Kate. I watch, fascinated, as the pulse in her neck throbs quickly with anticipation. I cover it with my mouth, sucking gently. Kate lifts her head and leans back.

"I've thought about this all day," I whisper against her skin. "Getting you here, getting you bare."

"So have I."

With one tug, the lace and satin pools around her feet, revealing my favorite playground. Kate steps over the dress and turns to me. Though I'm not a lingerie man, her undergarments are nothing short of beautiful. Blue silk with a white lace overlay—the bra strapless, the panties bikini, leading to sexy garters that keep opaque stockings in place.

There's wonder in Kate's voice as she says, "You're my husband." Then she smiles giddily. "How great is that?"

I chuckle. "It's pretty fucking awesome." I step purposefully to her. "And right now, your husband wants to sixty-nine his wife." I lick my lips. "A lot."

I loosen my tie and pull it off. But when I start with the buttons of my shirt, Kate's hand stops me. "Let me do it."

She watches her fingers as they reveal inch after inch of my heated skin. She opens my shirt, pushing it and my jacket down and off my arms. Then her hands run over my shoulders slowly, across my chest, down my abs.

In a husky voice she says, "I love your body, Drew. So strong, so hard . . . I could spend all night just touching you like this."

My heart pounds in my chest.

She opens my belt, the clasp of my pants. She crouches and kisses the happy trail. "And this right here"—her tongue traces the V of my upper pelvis, sculpted lines that show when sweats sit low on my hips—"this is my favorite part."

My breathing speeds up, and when her tongue goes back to teasing, I can't help but thrust forward, wanting it so frigging badly to be her I'm thrusting into.

Her mouth, her cunt . . . not choosy at the moment.

She drags my pants down my legs, and because of its proximity to Kate's mouth, my cock aches. Finally naked, I sit on the bed and crook my finger at Kate. "Come here."

She stands, and, keeping her bridal heels on, she struts to me. I grasp her hips; she braces one knee on the bed, straddling my waist. My hands move to her face, holding it still, and I kiss her roughly, sucking on her tongue, making her moan.

While I worship her mouth, Kate's hips gyrate, seeking friction. When she finds it against my dick, I grunt. Moving to her jaw and neck, I scour her skin with my lips and teeth—sucking and nibbling—while my deft fingers unclasp her bra from behind.

When her bra falls down, I lean back for the best view. "Jesus, your tits are beautiful." I take one in my palm, massaging and kneading, before bringing it to my mouth and suckling greedily.

Kate shouts nonsensical words and clasps my head to her breast. I lave at her nipple, then fall back on the bed, taking her with me. From this position, both of her tits are accessible—I take advantage and alternate between them—kissing and flicking each hard nipple with my tongue.

Full-out panting, Kate rears back and her eyes meet mine. I'm burning up, needing more—I can't remember ever being this desperate for her.

"Climb up here," I say. It's meant to be an order, but it comes out as a plea. "Right fucking here."

She rises to her knees and slides her panties and garters down and off. The heels follow. Then she crawls up the bed next to me, swings her knee around, and hovers over my insatiable mouth. Taking her hips in my hands, I guide her pussy down to my face.

She's so worked up, so hot, I feel the warmth against my lips even before I taste her. But when my tongue sinks inside, my eyes roll to the back of my head.

Her taste—fuck—it gets better every time. I revel in the sensation of being surrounded by her. I think she calls my name, but my heartbeat pulses so loud in my ears, I can't be sure. While I feast on her, Kate lowers her upper body so it's flush with my torso.

I feel her warm breath on my cock first. Then the sublime wetness of her mouth encases me—and I swear my heart stops in its tracks.

People who think this is wrong or depraved are out of their mind. If that were true, we wouldn't fit like this so fucking perfectly. We were made to do this.

My fingers dig into the flesh of her perfect ass. Holding her against me, moving her left and right in an unforgiving rhythm guaranteed to make her come. I want that so much—to feel her, my wife, pulsing around my tongue, writhing against my face.

She's not slow or teasing with her mouth now. She takes me all the way in, until I feel the back of her throat—then she sucks hard as she slides upward. Over and over, until my legs quake.

We work in tandem, giving and receiving the most salacious pleasure. She hums around me, and the vibrations push me closer to the edge. I feel the tingles in my spine, the tightening of my balls.

But I don't want to come like this—not yet. I'll certainly revisit that opportunity later, but this first time, I want to be buried deep inside her when I let go.

With renewed vigor, I find her clit with my tongue. I press against it, suck on it, then thrust inside her—stimulating all her pleasure points. When Kate starts to buck against me, when she loses her focus on my cock and has to take her mouth off it to get in enough air—I know my actions are about to pay off.

"Drew," she whimpers against my thigh, holding on to my

legs, trying to ground herself because she's about to take flight. I grasp her ass tighter. . . .

She's there. Falling. Flying. A thousand blissful eruptions coursing through her as she comes on my face and calls my name. Over and over.

Afterward, Kate stills and her harsh breaths tickle my thighs. Taking one last lick, I maneuver her boneless limbs until she's lying on the bed and I'm above her.

She smiles into my face, looking happy and orgasm-weak. "That was so good . . . the best ever."

I can only smirk as pure masculine pride wells in my chest. "The best . . . so far."

She lifts her arms around my neck, her knees bent and resting against my ribs. "Love me, Drew. Make love to me. Please."

I drag the tip of my cock up and down over her opening, savoring the feel of her hot wetness. "Look at me, Kate."

She gazes up at me—and I swear it feels like she's seeing into my soul. I push into her slowly, drawing the action out until our lower stomachs press together.

We're joined deeply—in every conceivable way.

My head tilts back and I shift my hips, moving in tight, close rotations. "You're so wet, Kate . . . you feel . . . Christ, it's unbelievable."

It really is.

In the last five years, I've wondered if sex between Kate and me would ever get stale. Ever not feel as if my blood vessels were exploding from pleasure overload.

Hasn't happened yet.

As far as I'm concerned, this cinches it. It's just going to keep getting better.

Her inner muscles contract and squeeze. At last I start to

move, dragging my dick out from her heavenly pussy, then thrusting back in. Groaning louder each time.

I lift up so I can watch. Nothing is more of a turn-on than watching my cock disappear into Kate. If I was going to go blind, that would be the last image I'd want to take into the darkness with me.

"Kiss me, Drew," she begs.

I lower my head and Kate's tongue runs across my lips, then plunges into my mouth—tangling with my own. Our hips move together, gaining speed and force. Our moans and whispered words mingle in our mouths and along the skin of our necks and shoulders.

This is more than magnificent screwing.

More than the physical expression of love.

It's spiritual.

I don't know if there's a heaven. I sure as shit don't know if I'll ever get there. But if there is . . . it's got to feel like this. Perfect harmony with another soul, surrounded by warmth and acceptance and rapture without end.

Amen.

Kate's hips rise to meet mine as I thrust into her again and again. Searing pleasure courses up my legs, threatening to burst, but I hold it off—because there's no way I'm going alone.

All I can pant out is "With me . . ."

Kate gasps, "Yes . . ."

I push in deep one last time and burst inside her in a forceful pulse. Spots dance behind my closed eyes, and exhilaration floods the motherfucking marrow of my bones. Kate constricts and throbs around me as her nails bite into my back.

After, neither of us moves for a few minutes. Not sure either of us can.

I finally manage to roll to the side, with my arms still around her—both of us breathing hard and slick with the best kind of sweat.

She brushes the damp hair off my forehead with a smile.

"Holy shit," I breathe. "That was incredible. We should've gotten married years ago."

"You said it. I think I had a stroke."

We laugh.

There are a few specific moments in my life that I consider as the greatest. That first night with Kate. The day she believed I loved her and told me she felt the same. The day James was born.

And this . . . this moment right here just made the list.

I pull her close and touch her face. My voice is rough, heavy with emotion, as the words are torn from my lungs. "I love you, Kate. I'm going to love you forever. And whatever comes after forever—I'm going to love you then too."

My words bring tears to her eyes, She kisses me gently, softly. Then she traces my lips with her finger. "You can bet your ass that I'm going to hold you to that, Drew Evans."

So that's it. The epic conclusion.

I think we've come a long away, don't you? From that guy you first met with the "flu," camped out on his living-room couch?

Boy, was he a fucking mess.

Thanks for sticking around, for not giving up on me. I know that at times you wanted to. But . . . it was great having you along for the ride.

If this were a fairy tale, now would be the time you'd read, "And they lived happily ever after . . ."

But that's just too boring for us.

So instead, I'll tell you this:

We lived . . . the same way we loved: with passion, tenderness, and laughter. And every day—every fucking day—to the very fullest.